ALSO BY RESHONDA TATE BILLINGSLEY
A Good Man Is Hard to Find
Say Amen, Again

ALSO BY VICTORIA CHRISTOPHER MURRAY
The Deal, the Dance, and the Devil
Sins of the Mother

BLUE ISLAND
PUBLIC LIBRARY

SINNERS
& Saints

VICTORIA
CHRISTOPHER MURRAY
and

RESHONDA
TATE BILLINGSLEY

A TOUCHSTONE BOOK
PUBLISHED BY SIMON & SCHUSTER
NEW YORK   LONDON   TORONTO   SYNDEY   NEW DELHI

BLUE ISLAND
PUBLIC LIBRARY

Touchstone
A Division of Simon & Schuster, Inc.
1230 Avenue of the Americas
New York, NY 10020

Copyright © 2012 by Victoria Christopher Murray and ReShonda Tate Billingsley

All rights reserved, including the right to reproduce this book or portions thereof in any form whatsoever. For information address Touchstone Subsidiary Rights Department, 1230 Avenue of the Americas, New York, NY 10020.

TOUCHSTONE and colophon are registered trademarks of Simon & Schuster, Inc.

Designed by Akasha Archer

Manufactured in the United States of America

ISBN 978-1-61793-502-2

A Note from
Victoria

This is the most difficult part of the writing process for me. Because now I have to talk about real people. My characters always do what I tell them to do (well, not always!). But real folks . . . whew; they get upset if you forget to mention their names. So in what has become my practice, I mention no one. If I love you, you already know it. If I like you, you know that, too. If I respect and admire you, I'm sure I've told you . . . and if I don't like you . . . well, I would never mention you anyway. So there, now I've covered everyone.

Now, on to those who could care less if they are mentioned or not. This has been by far the most fun I've had writing in the fourteen years that I've been blessed to do this. And it is completely because of ReShonda Tate Billingsley. Whew; Rachel worked nerves I didn't even know I had and ReShonda kept me on my toes. I took my game up because of her and I am so grateful that we fought for this project together. Thank you, ReShonda, for being such a great friend and writing partner. Can we just do this from now on? I am so glad that Trish Todd had the chance to edit this for us. Thank you, Trish, for believing in the project and for letting us know that you had a great time reading the story. Your edits stretched us and definitely made the story stronger. To Sulay Hernandez, I just didn't get enough time. But at least I get the chance to say thank you for coming to us at such a good time and for helping ReShonda and me to take this book up to a higher level. I had visions of you working with me on my next one hundred titles, but the best thing that came out of this connection is our friendship. To Shida Carr—there is only one word for you: The Best! Okay, that's two words, but you know what I mean. There is no one better in publicity. Period. Thank you for how you've helped build my career through the years. To the wonderful readers who stay with me year after year, novel after novel, we hope that you enjoy this one and will help ReShonda and me continue to pass the word. We write because of you!

And finally to my Lord and Savior, Jesus Christ. Whenever I think I'm too weary to walk this road anymore, you send a shining star. I just want to please you in all ways and I pray that my writing will continue to do just that. Thank you for guiding me as you see fit and for gifting me with a career that is my passion!

Peace,

Victoria

A Note from
ReShonda

As an avid reader, I was enthralled with the character Jasmine Larson Bush in Victoria Christopher Murray's Jasmine series. Not just because she was an intriguing, scandalous character, but because this little voice in my head kept saying, "Oh, I could *so* take that chick down."

That little voice belonged to one of my most popular characters—Rachel Jackson Adams from my Amen series. Rachel kept demanding that she and Jasmine meet.

That's why I was thrilled when Simon & Schuster gave us the go-ahead to make that meeting happen.

To say I loved writing this book with Victoria would be a serious understatement. This is the *most* fun I've ever had writing a book. Victoria is such a talented writer and I never knew what she would have Jasmine do next. That's the beauty of this collaboration. I'd write my chapter, and then sit back and wait to see how Miss Jasmine would work her way out of it. I literally would drop whatever I was doing when Victoria sent her chapters to me because I couldn't wait to see the story unfold.

I am thoroughly pleased with the result. So I hope you enjoy reading this book as much as we enjoyed writing it.

But before you get to reading about these two outrageous first ladies, please allow me a moment to thank those that made this journey possible. Of course, thank you, God, for your favor in allowing me to realize my writing dreams. Much love to my writing partner herself, Victoria Christopher Murray. You made this entire experience one I'll never forget.

To my family, who understood when I wanted to drop everything and write—my husband, Miron; mother, Nancy; sister, Tanisha; and my three beautiful kids. I appreciate your love and support. To my girl, Pat Tucker, thank you so much for not only allowing me to bounce scandalous scenarios off of you, but for always having my back.

As always, thanks to my agent, Sara Camilli, and to my team at Gallery Books: editor extraordinaire Brigitte Smith, my publicist Melissa Gramstad, and Louise Burke. Thank you to Trish Todd, Sulay Hernandez, and Shida Carr at Touchstone for all your hard work on shaping this into a final product that readers will love.

Thanks to the best literary assistant in the world! Kym Fisher, what would I do without you????

To my other literary friends, thanks for all of your support. You prove that we can all work together for a common goal—to get people reading: Nina Foxx, Kimberla Lawson Roby, Eric Jerome Dickey, Zane, Al Frazier, Dee Stewart, Tiffany Warren, Trice Hickman, Pat G'orge-Walker, J. D. Mason, and Rhonda McKnight.

Thank you to all the wonderful libraries, book clubs, churches, and schools that have supported my work. A big shout-out to my Facebook and Twitter families.

And finally thank you . . . yeah you, holding the book. Your support of this endeavor means the world to me. I hope you enjoy and we'd love to hear your feedback! Hit me up at www .reshondatatebillingsley.com.

Now . . . let's get ready to rumble!!

Much Love,
ReShonda

SINNERS
& Saints

Chapter ONE

How in the world was Jasmine going to keep her promise to God now?

Two years ago, she had promised Him that if He saved her daughter when she was kidnapped, if He brought her home safely, then she was going to live a life devoted just to Him. Jasmine had vowed that with Jacqueline's return, she was going to live the life that God had for her as Hosea's wife, as Jacqueline and Zaya's mother. She wasn't going to want for anything more than what God had given her, because surely, He had supplied her with enough.

God had done His part.

And for the last two years, Jasmine had done her part, too.

She'd lived a low-key life, thrilled that her greatest dramas were debates about fashion choices every morning with her seven-year-old daughter.

But how was she supposed to keep her promise to God now? After what her husband had just told her?

"So, hold up," Jasmine said, slipping into the chair across from Hosea. "I thought you were just going to the convention as the keynote speaker."

Hosea nodded.

"So, explain this to me again."

With a sigh, Hosea folded the newspaper he'd been reading and placed it on the table. He stuffed his mouth with a forkful of pancake, chewed for a moment, then said, "The call came in from a friend of Pop's, Pastor Earl Griffith. He thinks I need to submit my resume."

"To be the head of the American Baptist Coalition?"

Hosea nodded.

"But we're not Baptist."

His eyes danced with his amusement. "Get out of here."

"You know what I mean," Jasmine said, waving one hand. "I just don't get it. Why would they call you?"

"*They* didn't call me. Only Pastor Griffith. Seems like there're a couple of men in the running, though according to Griffith, the front-runner is Pastor Adams, Lester Adams from the Southern region."

Jasmine frowned. "I've never heard of him."

"Out of Houston. But Pastor Griffith doesn't think Adams is the man. Seems that the last four presidents have been from the South and Griffith and a couple of other pastors on the board think that the Coalition needs someone from the North, someone more progressive, to really move the organization forward."

"And they think that can be you?"

"Not *they,* darlin'. I told you—Griffith called me."

"But you said there were others who agreed with him."

Hosea nodded. "Apparently, they don't have anyone from the North who they think can go up against Adams. I guess they think my name could win this."

"That makes sense to me."

"It doesn't matter how much sense it makes, darlin'. I told Pastor Griffith that I'm not interested."

As if she didn't hear any of Hosea's last words, Jasmine whispered, "Wow." Old thoughts, familiar desires came to her mind—of power and prestige and money. How much money would a president receive?

She didn't know a lot about the American Baptist Coalition, but she knew enough. Like the fact that they were the largest African American religious organization, and wielded major political clout. And as much as black folks loved religion, the head of the ABC would have a boatload of power—and so would his wife.

Talk about being the first lady!

"Jasmine?"

I'd be the first lady of like . . . the world!

"Jasmine?"

"Huh?" Her eyes were glassy with images of her future and it took her a moment to focus on Hosea.

His admonishment came before he even said a word. It was in the way his eyes narrowed and the way he'd already begun shaking his head. "Don't even think about it."

"What?"

"You know what. I'm not gonna do it," he said slowly, as if he was speaking to one of their children. "I'm gonna go to the convention and speak, just like they asked. But I'm not gonna run for that office. The little I know about Lester Adams, he's a good man. They'll be fine with him."

"How could he be the one if I've never even heard of him?"

"Like you know every pastor in the country."

"I'm not talking about knowing every pastor. I'm thinking that Pastor Griffith is right. The head of the ABC should be someone who's known and who can add to the Coalition. Think about what you bring as the pastor of one of the largest churches in the country. Then, there's your show." She nodded. "Pastor Griffith is right," she repeated. "It has to be you."

His head was still shaking. "No. I don't want the drama."

"Who said anything about drama?"

"Any type of election—political or religious—is always about drama." He stood and placed his plate in the sink. "And then there's you, my wonderful wife. As much as I love you, darlin', anytime you're involved in anything, drama makes its way into our lives. No, I don't want any part of it."

"So, you're just gonna let this huge opportunity pass us—I mean, pass you by?"

"Yup, because it's not an opportunity that interests me. The church, the show, and most importantly you and the children are enough for me." He leaned over and kissed her forehead. "Speaking of the church, I'm gonna get dressed and head over there. I have a meeting in a couple of hours."

"Okay," she said, dismissing him with words, though she'd already dismissed him in her mind. Jasmine stayed as Hosea left her alone in the kitchen.

You and the children are enough for me.

Until a few minutes ago, she would've agreed with her husband. But this conversation was a game changer.

Hosea was right—their lives were without drama, but it had gotten kind of boring. Every day it was the same thing—getting the children off to school, then working on the women's committees at the church, then coming home to meet the children, then helping Mrs. Sloss with dinner, then . . . then . . . then . . .

Not that she had complaints; she loved her life, her family. But she would still love everyone, and maybe even a little bit more if Hosea were the head of the ABC.

Oh, no. She wasn't going to sit back and let this opportunity pass Hosea. He needed this position, even if he didn't know it.

Standing, she moved toward their bedroom, the conniving wheels of her brain already churning. She stood outside the door of their master bathroom, listening to her husband praise God, the spray of the shower, his accompanying music.

"I trust you, Lord!" He sang the words to one of Donnie McClurkin's songs.

"Babe," she said, interrupting his praise time. "I'm gonna run over to Mae Frances's apartment, okay?"

"Don't you have a meeting at the church?"

"Yeah, but it's not till this afternoon and Mae Frances just called and she really needs me to help her with something." Jasmine paused. It had been a long time since she'd manipulated the truth to get something she wanted. But it wasn't like she was going back to being a total liar again—she just needed to get this done and after Hosea was in his rightful place, she'd go back to being on the side of righteousness.

"Oh, okay. Is Nama all right?" he asked, referring to Mae Frances by the name their children called the older woman.

"She's fine. You know Nama. I'll call Mrs. Whittingham and tell her that I may be a little late for my meeting."

By the time they said their good-byes and Jasmine grabbed her purse, she already had a plan. But she'd need some help, and Mae Frances, her friend who knew everyone from Al Sharpton to Al Capone and his offspring, was just the person to help her.

"Sorry, Pastor Adams," she said to herself as she rode down in the elevator. "Whoever you are, you can be the president of the ABC once Hosea and I are done—in, say, ten or twenty years."

She stepped outside of their Central Park South apartment building and into the New York springtime sun. Slapping on her designer glasses, she laughed out loud.

Oh, yeah, today was gonna be a really good day.

Chapter TWO

Watch out, Michelle Obama!

Rachel Jackson Adams smiled in satisfaction as she surveyed her reflection in the bathroom mirror. She'd had to leave the prestigious American Baptist Coalition regional dinner and step inside the restroom to compose herself. After all, she was about to be the first lady of one of the most prestigious organizations in the country. She couldn't very well be acting a plumb fool because she was overcome with excitement. But Rachel had wanted to do a backflip, front flip, toe touch, cartwheel, and anything else she could think of to express her joy.

Rachel fluffed her honey brown curls, then lightly refreshed her MAC Oh Baby lip gloss. She had come such a long way. Her mother was probably dancing in her grave at the sight of Rachel as not only a first lady, but a soon-to-be prominent one at that. Rachel had worked hard to garner the respect of the parishioners at Zion Hill Missionary Baptist Church. She'd grown up in that church, so everyone knew her dirt—all of it—and it had taken God himself to get these people to respect her. And while Zion Hill had grown tremendously, it still wasn't considered a megachurch, and outside of Houston there were few who had even heard of it. As the first lady of the American Baptist Coalition, her status would go to a whole new level. Shoot, if she had to be first lady, she might as well be the *top* first lady.

Rachel savored the thought as she dropped her lip gloss back into her clutch and stepped back into the corridor.

"I was beginning to think you'd fallen in," her husband of eight years said before leaning in and lightly kissing Rachel on the cheek.

Lester Adams wasn't her true love—that title belonged to her thirteen-year-old son's father, Bobby Clark. But Lester was good *for* her. Her love for Lester was that agape love they talked about in First Corinthians. It brought out the best in her. Well, for the most part anyway. Life with Bobby had been filled with drama—Rachel admitted much of that was her own doing, but it was drama-filled nonetheless. And although Bobby still remained a part of Jordan's life, Rachel had finally gotten him out of her system and was focusing all of her attention on making her marriage work.

"What took you so long?" Lester asked, snapping Rachel out of her thoughts.

"Sorry," Rachel said with a slight smile, "but you know I'm about to be the preeminent first lady, so I had to make sure my makeup was on point." She tossed her hair back. "Come to think of it, I think I'll change my name to Lady Rachel so I can have the title to go along with the position."

Lester narrowed his eyes and glared at his wife. "Rachel," he began in that voice she hated—the one that he always used when he was chastising her.

"What?" Rachel shrugged, already getting defensive.

"I don't have the position yet," he said matter-of-factly. "The regional board just nominated me tonight. There's still a national election."

Rachel waved him off. "That's just a formality. Did you hear those election results? You beat Pastor Johnson seventy-three to twenty-five percent!"

Lester sighed. "Pastor Johnson also got his sixteen-year-old stepniece pregnant." As soon as Lester said it, he looked like he wished he could take the words back.

The smile immediately left Rachel's face. Lester was no saint himself. He'd had his own little pregnant-woman-on-the-side debacle. But thank God, they'd worked through that crisis.

"I'm just saying," Lester quickly continued, like he wanted to prevent Rachel's mind from traveling down that rocky memory lane, "Pastor Johnson wasn't that hard to beat. I still have to run against whomever they nominate from the North region, and rumor has it they're bringing out their top dog—Pastor Hosea Bush."

"That jack-legged TV preacher?" Rachel asked with a frown.

Lester shook his head. "Pastor Bush is not jack-legged. He's well established, comes from a highly respected family, and he leads one of the largest churches in the country."

"*So?* He's. Not. You," Rachel said, reaching up and adjusting Lester's bow tie. Lester had been an extreme nerd when they were in high school—which is why Rachel had never given him the time of day. But he'd pursued her relentlessly and eventually had worn her down. He was willing to be a father to her two kids and he loved her unconditionally. So she agreed to give their relationship a try, but not before having him shave off that red mop of a hairstyle he wore and introducing him to Proactiv. She'd revamped his wardrobe, taught him how to have a little swagger, and now, even she had to admit, he had it going on. Not to mention the fact that he was an awesome preacher. "Lester, sweetheart," Rachel said, taking her husband's hands, "you heard that emcee tonight. For the past sixty years, the president of the ABC has been a Southerner. That's not about to change. I don't care how prominent this Rev. Tree is."

Lester let out a small chuckle. "Pastor *Bush,*" he corrected.

"Tree, Bush, Leave, whatever," she said, flicking her hand. "The bottom line is, that position is ours. God said so."

He laughed again. "Oh, God said so, huh?"

Rachel nodded emphatically. "He sure did. And if God said it, then it's so." She grinned widely.

"Look at my baby," Lester said proudly. "And to think, you threatened to divorce me for entering the ministry."

"Well, that's because I'd spent my life as a preacher's daughter. I wasn't trying to be a preacher's wife. But I've gotten the hang of it now."

"You do make a great first lady," Lester said, kissing her again. "And can I say it again—you look lovely in that dress."

"Thank you. And I'm going to make an even better first lady on a national level." She tightened the belt on her royal blue Diane von Furstenberg silk dress. Her attire tonight was just one indication of how far she'd come. Just a few years ago, she would've shown up to an event like this in the latest Baby Phat or Apple Bottoms style that she could find. And although she still loved her some Kimora Lee Simmons, she didn't have to wear it *everywhere*.

"Congratulations, Rev. Adams," an elderly man said as he walked past them.

Lester stopped and smiled. "Thank you, sir."

"I can't wait until you officially claim that presidency," the man said as he stepped on to the elevator.

"From your lips to God's ears," Lester replied as he waved good-bye.

Rachel waited for the elevator door to close. "See, everyone knows you're the man for the job. And I'm the woman that needs to be next to the man for the job."

"Since when did this kind of stuff excite you?"

Rachel's hands went to her hips. "Since I did my homework. Do you know that the last wife of the ABC president was invited everywhere? To White House dinners, commencement ceremonies, the Grammys—she even cohosted on *The View*!"

"But wasn't she a TV journalist anyway?"

Rachel frowned. Lester and all this negativity was about to work her nerves. "That's beside the point. Everyone knows the ABC president is one of the most powerful men in the country, so that means the ABC's president's wife would be one of the most powerful women."

"I'm just saying, don't get ahead of yourself."

"Whatever, Lester." Rachel rolled her eyes. She'd been euphoric since they announced he'd won the election an hour ago. Of course, she always knew he would, but hearing it confirmed was the icing on the cake.

As thoughts of hanging out with Michelle Obama danced in her head, Rachel once again smiled.

"Rachel, I see your mind working."

"Just trying to determine where I'll get my dress for your induction ceremony." Maybe she could get Kimora to design her something personally.

"Rachel—"

She put her finger to his lips. "Shhhh," she said, draping her arm through his. "Let's just savor the moment tonight. Let's go back in, mingle with the people, and enjoy ourselves. My dad and Brenda have the kids, so the night is all ours. Tomorrow, we'll talk about the national election." Rachel decided to just change the subject because she didn't care what Lester said, he *would* win the national election. And if this Reverend Bush proved to be a problem, well, Rachel might just have to revert to her old bag of tricks—just for a moment—to make sure that he wasn't a threat. She wasn't going to let anything, or anyone, stand in the way of claiming what was destined to be hers.

Chapter THREE

Not even the deep breath she took could stop Jasmine's knees from knocking; this was really happening. She wiggled her butt against the wooden chair in the Langston Hughes Auditorium, but it was difficult to get comfortable, especially since she couldn't stop shaking.

"You all right, darlin'?" Hosea squeezed her hand.

She could only give him a nod before her glance wandered again to the men in front of the stage. Their heads were bowed together, their voices low. Jasmine strained, wanting to take in even a single syllable of what they were saying. But it was impossible to hear their whispers through the chatter of the two hundred or so participants in the room.

She pressed her knees together. It wasn't that she was nervous—this was all excitement. Because this was the day she'd been waiting for . . . the voting for the pastor who would represent the Northern region in the national election for president of the American Baptist Coalition. The region had actually postponed the election for more than three weeks under the guise of opening the ballot to more pastors. But though several had submitted their resumes, only Hosea's had been accepted to go up against the four other pastors whose names were already on the ballot.

Now, just weeks after Hosea had declared that he would never run for president of the esteemed organization, Jasmine, Hosea, the Senior Reverend Bush, and a host of friends from their church filled the first two rows of the auditorium waiting for what Pastor Griffith had called the inevitable.

And this was all happening because of her.

Just like with everything else in their lives, she had taken charge, knowing what was best for her husband, even when he didn't have a clue.

She hadn't done it alone, though—no, a task like this had taken big names, big guns. It had taken Mae Frances. And her connections.

For the last eight years, every time Jasmine needed to win, her friend had handled it, had worked it out, had brought the victory home. And this time was no different . . .

"I agree, Jasmine Larson," Mae Frances had said the morning Jasmine had barreled into her apartment, telling her that she needed her like never before. "This position would be wonderful for Preacher Man," she said, calling Hosea by the nickname she'd given him when they'd met all those years ago. "And"—she paused for a moment—"this will be great for you."

Not more than the beat of a second passed before Jasmine said, "And anything that's good for me will be good for you."

Mae Frances had reared back on the sofa that Hosea and Jasmine had given her, and released a hearty laugh. "You got that right. I always gets mine." She was still chuckling, but then turned to her serious get-down-to-business tone. "So, tell me what you know."

The two had moved to the mahogany dining room table, this piece of furniture a gift to Mae Frances from Hosea's father, Rev. Samuel Bush. And as Jasmine leaned forward and relayed to Mae Frances everything that Hosea had told her, Mae Frances took notes as if making things happen was her job.

"So, that's it?" Mae Frances asked when Jasmine stopped after two minutes.

Jasmine nodded. "I don't even know that pastor—Griffith. I never heard of him before this morning."

Mae Frances frowned a little. "I wonder if that's Earl Griffith out of Chicago."

Jasmine shook her head. Was there anyone her friend didn't know?

"I don't know where he's from," Jasmine said. "All I know is that he called and he wants Hosea to run . . . and I do, too. I want him to have that position . . . I need him to be the president."

"Whoa! Hold on, Jasmine Larson." Mae Frances held up her hands. "Calm down. You've been home being the good wife for the last couple of years and it shows. You talking like you've forgotten how to play this game."

Jasmine's frown asked her question.

"You're acting like you've already hit the home run. The old Jasmine would know that you can't get too far out in front—you've got to touch first, second, and third base before you can bring it home." Mae Frances continued, "So, back to the business of getting Preacher Man to be the leader of the—"

"Not the leader, the president."

"Whatever! You want him to be the head Negro in charge, right?"

Jasmine cringed at her friend's choice of words, but still, she nodded. No one had ever accused Mae Frances of being loaded with class. But no one could deny that for an assignment like this, there was only one person who could make it happen . . . and that was exactly what Mae Frances had done.

She had sent Jasmine home with no information, but no worries, either, and by the time Jasmine maneuvered the thirty or so blocks from the Upper East Side to Central Park South, Mae Frances's plan was already in motion.

It hadn't even been a half hour from when she left Mae Frances until she stepped into her apartment, but when Jasmine walked inside, Hosea had not yet left to go to his office in the church. He was still at home, pacing the length of their living room, his cell phone pressed against his ear. With his eyebrows bunched together, and his forehead creased with deep wrinkles, Jasmine knew that the talk was serious—she knew it was about the ABC.

"I hear you, Steve," Hosea said as Jasmine laid her purse on the table.

Ah, she thought. So that's where Mae Frances had started. She'd begun with Hosea's award-winning cable talk show. Steven Hager was the executive producer of *Bring It On,* and because of his and Hosea's efforts, the show enjoyed ratings that rivaled some network programs. *Bring It On* was Hosea's cherished project, his idea, his success. And Jasmine knew what Mae Frances knew—that Hosea would do anything to help the show thrive even more.

Jasmine peeked into the living room from the foyer and waved to Hosea, letting him know that she had returned. But he'd only nodded, distracted by his conversation. She pretended to have her own distraction, glancing through yesterday's mail, which she'd already sorted. But though her eyes were turned away, her ears were at full attention.

"Yeah, it would be great for the show, but if I were going to take a position like that, it would have to be for much more than just good ratings," Hosea said, still pacing.

Then more silence, peppered every few seconds with Hosea grunting, "Uh-huh, uh-huh." Then something on the other end of the line made Hosea stop. Made his eyes widen. Made him sit down . . . slowly.

Jasmine's heart pounded.

"You're kidding me?" he whispered. "Jeremiah Wright?"

Jasmine pressed her lips together, but it was still hard to keep the scream inside. It pressed through her lips—a little yelp—just enough to make Hosea look up and at her for just a moment.

"Well, yeah," Hosea said. "If he thinks I should do it . . . if he thinks I can bring something to the Coalition."

There was more silence, but at the mention of Jeremiah

Wright's name, Jasmine knew that Mae Frances had hit that home run. Hosea might say no to Pastor Griffith, and even no to her. But not to the man whom he considered a stand-up guy, a hero, a mentor, even though he'd never met him.

"Okay," Hosea said. "Yeah, definitely give Reverend Wright my number." His voice was filled with an excitement that Jasmine had not heard in a while. "I'll call Pastor Griffith back now."

Hosea hung up and turned to a nonchalant Jasmine. "You are not going to believe this."

"What?" she asked, her eyes still on the mail.

"Jeremiah Wright."

"Oh, did you speak to him?" When Hosea frowned, Jasmine realized that maybe she was being a bit too casual. So she added, "Really?" as if she were surprised.

It was enough to get Hosea back on track. "No, I didn't speak to him, but he called Steve over at the studio. He said he heard that the ABC was considering me and that he'd followed me and the show after all that we went through with Jacquie." He paused and sat down on the sofa. "He really wants me to run and represent the North in the national election."

"Babe, that's great!" This time, Jasmine didn't have to add anything to her voice. Her excitement was enough. "So, if Reverend Wright is taking an interest in this, then . . ."

She left the sentence open for Hosea to finish. "Then, I have to do it." He nodded. "I don't have any choice." Glancing at Jasmine, he smiled as he stood up. "I need to make another call. I'm going to call back Pastor Griffith."

Within an hour, Hosea had reneged on his promise to never run and had faxed his resume to Pastor Griffith. An hour after that, Hosea Bush's name was on the ballot to represent the Northern region.

From that point, it was a done deal. Three candidates who'd been in the running dropped out—very quietly, but quickly. Only a single pastor, Reverend Penn, remained. William Penn, a sixty-seven-year-old small-time pastor, was the leader of New

Hope Baptist in Springfield Gardens, Queens. New Hope was Pastor Penn's seventh church, and interestingly, he'd had as many wives, changing spouses every time he was moved to a new congregation for one reason (or scandal) or another.

But while the Northern board had been able to convince the other pastors to step away, no one had been able to persuade Reverend Penn to do the same.

"This is my rightful position," the reverend had complained when he found out that Hosea was now in the running. "I've been trying to be president for the last twenty-three years!" He'd whined and stomped his foot like a child, but no one listened—no one except for his thirty-eight-years-younger wife, a synthetic-hair-weave-wearing leggy blonde who'd left her porn career behind when she married the pastor.

When Jasmine had first heard that Reverend Penn refused to drop out, she'd had Mae Frances pull a dossier on the Penns. But then she'd met the pitiful couple and told Mae Frances to forget it. If justice didn't prevail, if Hosea couldn't beat this false prophet and his trick of a wife, then he didn't deserve this position.

"So, the votes are in."

The voice of Pastor Griffith dragged Jasmine away from the memories of the past weeks. She smiled at the pastor, and did her best to have only pure thoughts about the sexiest preacher that she'd ever seen. Pastor Griffith (yes, Earl Griffith; yes, a connection of Mae Frances's) may have been a man of the cloth from Chicago, but if he'd ever decided to walk away and onto the stage, any movie producer would gladly scoop him right up. Even though he was in his sixties, he had the suaveness of that back-in-the-day actor Billy Dee Williams, and the swagger of President Barack Obama. Jasmine was in love—or she would have been, had she not been married and loved Hosea so much.

As if he felt her stare, Pastor Griffith glanced over at Jasmine and granted her a small smile.

She sighed like a teenager.

"You okay, darlin'?"

Jasmine had to shake her head a little, to take her eyes off of Pastor Griffith. "What?" she said, turning to her husband. "Oh. Yeah. I'm fine." This time, she squeezed Hosea's hand, but turned her eyes back to Pastor Griffith.

It wasn't just his amazing looks that made Jasmine admire the man. It was the way he did business. As the Northern director, Pastor Griffith was in charge. So, he had changed the election date to give the membership time to read about, and get to know, Hosea. And then, he'd told her and Hosea that there wasn't a single thing to worry about.

"It's gonna go down the way I want it to go down," he'd said in his deep, melodic, Barry White voice.

Hosea hadn't been pleased, always wanting to do everything by the good book. But Jasmine had melted. Pastor Griffith's words, the way he handled things, were as pleasing as the sound of his voice.

Now Pastor Griffith cleared his throat, adjusted the microphone, and said, "By a vote of ninety-three to seven percent, Pastor Hosea Bush will represent the Northern region in the national election for president of the American Baptist Coalition."

The applause was strong and loud; there was hope in the cheers as so many saw Hosea Bush as their first real chance of victory in more than sixty years.

Hosea stood and hugged Jasmine. But while there was nothing but smiles all around as the entire City of Lights assembly congratulated Hosea, Jasmine's face was pinched with a scowl.

Ninety-three to seven? Who had the nerve to vote against Hosea?

"Well, congratulations, Pastor Bush."

Reverend Penn's scratchy voice infiltrated their celebration. "It was a hard-fought fight," the reverend said.

No, it wasn't. The only reason Jasmine kept that thought inside was because Pastor Griffith had stepped down from the podium to offer his own congratulations—and she needed him to know that she was a proper—the perfect—first lady.

"Thank you, Reverend Penn." Hosea responded with a slight bow, gracious, as always. "I hope that I'll have your support when we get to Los Angeles."

"Of course, of course," Reverend Penn said. Though his words were positive, his tone told them all that he wasn't going to do a damn thing.

"And you can count on my support, too." The reverend's wife swung her waist-long fake hair so hard over her shoulder that both Reverend Bush and Pastor Griffith, who were standing behind her, ducked. "We definitely want one of our own to win finally," she purred, with her lips and her chest poked out.

His wife sounded way more sincere than her husband, and Jasmine wondered if she would have been as affable in defeat. But then all good thoughts of the woman evaporated when Mrs. Penn licked her full, ruby-red-colored lips. With her eyes planted on Hosea, she said, "I'll do whatever I can to help you win, Pastor Bush. *Whatever!*"

Jasmine could almost feel Hosea hold his breath when she jumped in front of the ex–porn star. But he didn't have a thing to worry about. She wasn't going to act like a crazy fool—not in the Langston Hughes Auditorium. Not in front of all the people who were going to work to get her husband elected.

Jasmine simply reached for the woman's hand. "Thank you. Hosea and I are both looking forward to working with you." A smile was on Jasmine's face, but she held the woman's hand even after she stopped talking. Squeezed it a little, then stepped back. Her eyes stayed glued to Mrs. Penn. *Don't mess with me,* Jasmine told the woman telepathically.

From one man-stealer to another, the message was received. Mrs. Penn stumbled back, turned away, and scurried out of the room like she was being chased.

Hmph! Jasmine grinned; it was good to know that she still had it.

"Well," Pastor Griffith said, "I guess we all need to get home and do some packing."

"Yes, definitely," the senior Bush said. "We just have a week to get ready for Los Angeles."

And a week after that, I'll be first lady to every African American Christian in America. And Hosea will be president, too.

The victorious group edged up the aisle. But as everyone talked about their plans, Jasmine had no time to participate in the petty chatter. Her thoughts were on Mae Frances.

It was so unlike her friend to miss an occasion like this. And Hosea had been disappointed when Mae Frances had called that morning and told him that she wasn't feeling well. But that had been the lie that Jasmine and Mae Frances had conjured up. The truth was that her friend had stayed home because she had much work to do. Pastor Griffith had assured them that Hosea had this election—there was no need for any last-minute manipulations. So, Mae Frances had stayed home to move forward to phase two.

"Babe, I'm gonna go check on Mae Frances," Jasmine said, once they all stood outside.

"Oh. But Pops wants to take us out to dinner for a celebration."

"Yeah, I figured we'd head over to Sylvia's," Hosea's father added.

"I'm sorry, but I really want to make sure she's okay," Jasmine said, her face pinched with concern for their friend. "Being that she's home alone and everything."

"Yeah, you're right. Go on." Hosea kissed her. "I'll bring a plate home for you."

"That would be great," Jasmine said, already rushing to a cab that'd stopped in front of the group.

She blew Hosea a kiss before she gave the driver Mae Frances's address. Then she leaned back and closed her eyes.

Okay, they'd gotten to first base. Really, second and third base, too. Now Jasmine wanted to know how they were going to hit that grand-slam home run.

Jasmine couldn't wait to see her friend. She couldn't wait to find out what the plan was to make sure that Hosea won the national election.

She couldn't wait to hear how they were going to bring Pastor Lester Adams down!

didn't need to be up in this suite ranting; she and Mae Frances needed to get downstairs to set the rest of this day in motion.

"I'd almost forgotten," Jasmine said, turning to the mirror. She finger-fluffed her curls, then reached for her makeup kit. "You think we can really pull this off?"

Mae Frances glanced at Jasmine in the mirror and smirked. "We're dealing with Rachel Adams, aren't we? She's young and dumb. She's so eager to impress these women that she's going to jump at the bait. Trust me."

That's just what Jasmine wanted to hear. She clicked off the light in the bathroom, turned to Mae Frances, and said, "Let's roll."

In the hallway, Mae Frances gave Jasmine the folder that she'd prepared last night; these would be the last moments Jasmine had to study. Once the elevator came, their talking ceased and they rode down in silence. The elevator stopped on almost every floor as the first ladies made their way to the biggest event of the week for the women. Along the way, Jasmine was greeted with pleasant smiles and a few congratulations, but the soft chatter was all about Rachel Adams and Regina West.

Jasmine sighed. After this morning's session, she'd expected the women to be groveling at her feet, ready to crown her queen.

But there was no need to sweat this. In just a couple of hours, she'd be the one back on top—where she deserved to be. And Rachel? Well, the women of the American Baptist Coalition would realize that Rachel was nothing more than a ghetto-not-so-fabulous street girl who couldn't stand next to her, or any of them, no matter how many lies she told.

As the women filed from the elevator into the hall leading to the Grand Ballroom, Jasmine and Mae Frances pressed through the crowd as politely as they could. At the door, they paused, and with eagle eyes they scanned the massive space. In moments, Jasmine zoomed in on Cecelia King. She was in the center, as always, her majesty surrounded by her royal court. But this time she wasn't alone. Rachel Adams stood at her side as if she were the princess preparing to take her rightful place.

Jasmine had to take a breath. Rachel was standing where she was supposed to be.

"This is better for the plan," Mae Frances whispered, as if she knew Jasmine's thoughts. "Just go on up in there, do it the way I told you, and I'll handle phase two." She patted the envelope she held in her hand, then gently pushed Jasmine forward.

Jasmine sauntered toward the group in the center, as if she wasn't in a hurry. But each passing second pulled them closer to the start of the program and Jasmine had to make this happen right now.

There was a crowd around Cecelia and Rachel, and if she hadn't had a plan, Jasmine would be fuming again. But she delighted in the fact that it wouldn't be long before Rachel was flat on her face.

How am I going to get Cecelia's attention? Jasmine thought. But there was no need for her concern. The moment Jasmine caught Cecelia's gaze, the older woman smiled. With a nod, Jasmine beckoned her, as if she had something important to share.

"Excuse me, ladies," Cecelia said before she stepped toward Jasmine.

But as Cecelia moved away from the group, Rachel did, too, as if she'd been invited to join Jasmine's discussion.

It was rude . . . it was immature . . . and it played right into Jasmine's hand.

Cecelia spoke first. "I didn't get a chance to tell you before, but I wanted to say what an awesome testimony you gave at the reception. What you want to do for the ladies of the American Baptist Coalition, and the whole country really, is simply amazing."

"Thank you." Jasmine lowered her eyes properly, as if the compliment was too much. "I just want to do what I can to make sure no mother has to go through what I did."

"Oh, yeah," Rachel said. "What you did up there was really special. A million dollars, huh?"

Both Jasmine and Cecelia stared at Rachel for a moment, letting her know her comment was inappropriate. "Rachel, honey," Cecelia began in a teacher's tone. "This has nothing to do with money. Her child was taken away and violated. Don't you know that?"

"Yeah, but . . ."

Cecelia sighed as if she was exasperated. "This offer came from Jasmine's heart, to protect other children and other parents." To Jasmine, Cecelia said, "You are to be commended for going through and coming through that. And to stand up there and share it with all of us . . ." She pressed her hand against her chest, shook her head, then pulled Jasmine into her arms.

Over Cecelia's shoulder, Jasmine saw Rachel roll her eyes. Oh, yeah. This was gonna be fun. It was time to take the wench down.

"Thank you so much," Jasmine said, pulling back. "And I wanted to thank you for introducing me at the reception." She paused, glanced at Rachel, who stood in place as if she had no intention of leaving Cecelia's side. "I'm hoping, Cecelia, that you'll let me return the favor. I'm sure there is someone already assigned to introduce you, but"—she hoped this was the part that would get Rachel—"since the women have already met me and are really getting to know me now, which is positive for my husband, I'm hoping you'll give me a chance to make a few more points . . . and introduce you."

"Oh . . . well . . . that's an idea." Cecelia lowered her head as if she was pondering the suggestion.

"It would mean a lot to me." Jasmine glanced at Rachel, who stood now, with her arms folded, with her eyes squinted, as if she was in deep thought. But Rachel hadn't jumped in yet, so it was time for Jasmine to go in for the kill. "It would mean a lot to Hosea . . . if you know what I mean." Jasmine shared a chuckle with Cecelia.

Rachel stepped in—literally. With her elbow, she nudged Jasmine aside. Any other time, Jasmine would've knocked the trollop upside her head. But she stepped back and allowed Rachel to fall into her trap. "Ummm . . . Cecelia, really, I would love to introduce you." Turning to Jasmine, she added, "I mean, you've already had a chance to speak to the women and many of them don't know who I am. So, I would love the opportunity and I think it's only fair . . ." She paused, then added, "And I'm sure you don't want it to look like you're favoring one of us over the other."

Fool! Jasmine thought as Cecelia's eyes narrowed at Rachel's words.

"I mean," Rachel began, as if she knew she had to clean this up, "I would never say that, but I heard some of the other ladies talkin'."

Jasmine was sure that Rachel was going to ruin her plan if she kept on, so she jumped in. "You know what? That's probably a good idea. Rachel, you should introduce Cecelia." Both looked at Jasmine as if they didn't believe her. Jasmine added, "I mean, you've been so gracious to me, Cecelia, and I don't want Rachel to feel bad . . ."

"I don't feel bad," Rachel said with too much attitude. "I'm just sayin'. . ."

Would you shut up? Jasmine wanted to scream. *You're going to ruin my plan!*

For a moment, Cecelia stared hard at Jasmine, as if she suspected that Jasmine didn't have a polite bone in her body— that this had to be part of some kind of trick or scheme. But finally, Cecelia relented. "Are you sure you're okay with this, Jasmine?"

"Absolutely!"

Cecelia motioned toward the tall, lanky woman who'd been following her around since they'd arrived. Though Cecelia never introduced her to anyone, Jasmine was sure she was her assistant.

Cecelia whispered something to her friend that neither Jasmine nor Rachel could hear. When they moved apart, the woman motioned for Rachel to follow her.

With a smirk and a "Hmph," Rachel sashayed away, putting way too much swing in her hips, as if she'd forgotten where she was.

Cecelia shook her head slightly, and frowned as she watched Rachel saunter away.

But Jasmine was all smiles. *Some people are just perfect victims, perfect idiots!*

This was one of those good news—bad news scenarios. The good news was that as the wife of one of the top contenders for the position of president, Jasmine was placed on the dais next to Cecelia King. The bad news—on the other side of Cecelia was Rachel, who did her best to keep Cecelia engaged and away from Jasmine throughout the entire program.

Even after lunch had been served, Rachel never stopped talking. It was only when a short break was announced before dessert and the women stood to mingle that she finally shut up.

When Cecelia stepped away and Jasmine and Rachel were alone, Rachel said, "You know, Jasmine, when Lester is voted in as president, I'm sure he can find a place for your husband to work for him." She pushed her chair back from the table and stood. "In fact, I may ask you to do a few little things for me, too." She laughed softly as she swung her fake Gucci purse that was a perfect match to the Kmart special dress she wore, and stepped down from the dais.

Jasmine's eyes followed Rachel as she sauntered through the crowd, stopping here and there, roaming to and fro . . . just like Satan. She kept her eyes on Rachel as she left the ballroom, obviously on her way to the restroom to freshen up for her grand introduction.

And then Jasmine's eyes wandered to the folder that Rachel had left beside her place setting. In the next instant, Mae Frances joined her on the stage, but neither woman said a word to the other. With the slightest movement, Mae Frances exchanged the manila folder at Rachel's seat with one that she held. Then she left the stage just as quickly as she came.

By the time Rachel returned, Jasmine was shivering with anticipation. When the mistress of ceremonies quieted the group, the women settled at their seats for coffee, tea, and dessert . . . and to hear from their leader, First Lady Cecelia King.

"It is my honor," the mistress of ceremonies began, "to present Mrs. Rachel Adams, who will introduce our keynote speaker."

The applause was polite as Rachel pushed back her chair, grabbed the folder with the bio, and then took her time strolling to the podium.

Rachel stood for a moment, her shoulders back, her head high—with much more poise than Jasmine expected. And for the briefest of moments, Jasmine wondered if Rachel was going to be able to pull this off. Would she scan the paper ahead of time, or would she just read, knowing that she'd already reviewed the bio?

But then Jasmine calmed herself. There was no way Rachel would be smart enough to glance over the sheet once again. The truth was, even she would just get up there and start reading if she were in Rachel's position.

Rachel opened her mouth and Jasmine took a breath. "Thank you all so much. It is such a pleasure to be here and to introduce a woman whom I've admired from afar for many years."

Jasmine raised an eyebrow. Afar? Impressive. She'd expected Rachel to just go up there, stutter a bit, and then start reading.

Rachel said, "As many of you may know, my father, Simon Jackson, has been the pastor of Zion Hill for many years. And if I've learned one thing from him, it's that our leaders are important because they are the ones who help us set the tone to bring others to Christ. So, Lady Cecelia, thank you for setting a wonderful tone for all of us to follow."

The applause was a little louder this time and Jasmine had to release a long breath. Where was this coming from? Rachel Adams sounded like she had a little bit of class. Was she ever going to open that folder? Was she ever going to read what Mae Frances had prepared?

Rachel cleared her throat, leaned closer to the microphone,

then did what Jasmine had been expecting—she began to read. "Cecelia King wasn't always a first lady. In fact, few know that she was a wildcat often found butt-naked . . . in college . . ." She paused as her eyes scanned the page.

Gasps and the clanking of dropped forks filled the air. Followed by whispers and glares.

"Oh, my God," Rachel said, though no one in the room heard her.

The chatter grew louder as the women stared and pointed, their disgust palpable.

The moments that passed had to feel like minutes to Rachel as she looked from side to side, not knowing what to do.

Jasmine jumped from her seat and rushed to Rachel's side. She put her arm around Rachel's shoulder and spoke into the microphone. "Obviously, there's been a mistake," Jasmine said. "But together, Rachel and I can tell you about the real Cecelia King. The woman who was raised in Smackover, Arkansas, who's been working since she was fourteen years old. The woman who helped her mother raise her six brothers and sisters while she put herself through the University of Arkansas at Fayetteville."

Jasmine continued the litany of Cecelia's accomplishments, never looking down at a single paper and never letting go of Rachel. This was the important part, Mae Frances had told her. The women had to see them side by side.

"The Bible tells us how important a helpmate is," Jasmine continued, "and it is because of Cecelia King that her husband, Reverend Andre King, has held the position of president of the American Baptist Coalition for eight years."

She paused as the women applauded.

Jasmine said, "But she leaves her own legacy with the National Head Start program that she initiated, along with the Reading Is Fundamental book drives that occur all over the country because of her vision."

More applause, and this time Jasmine paused long enough to take in the crowd. Rachel's blunder was not forgotten, but in their eyes Jasmine could see that the women were impressed with her. She was snapping off Cecelia's accomplishments as if she'd been by Cecelia's side for every one of them—and without reading from any notes whatsoever. And Rachel had to continue standing silently next to her, Jasmine's protective arm still around her shoulder—the princess and the pauper.

"And to quote one of Lady Cecelia's favorite scriptures . . ." Jasmine paused. She had no idea if this was Cecelia's favorite scripture or not, but Mae Frances had said with the way that woman went around quoting the Bible, they could pick out anything and it would work. Jasmine said, "For the Lord is great and greatly to be praised. Ladies, let us praise the Lord for our first lady! Without any further ado . . . or mix-ups"—she paused at the laughter and felt Rachel stiffen beneath her hold—"I bring to you the first lady of all first ladies, Mrs. Cecelia King."

This time, the women rose to their feet, but as Cecelia walked past Rachel and hugged Jasmine, Jasmine knew that the ovation was as much for her as it was for Cecelia.

When Cecelia finally leaned back and caught her eye, Jasmine took a quick breath. It was the smirk that Cecelia wore that made Jasmine wonder—it was a smirk that said she knew Jasmine was behind this whole setup.

Well, so what? Of course, she probably knew. But even if Cecelia suspected that, it didn't matter. Jasmine's goal was to please many more than Cecelia King. There were many other first ladies who had to be impressed with her, and the reaction from the other women just moments before told her that she'd accomplished her goals.

Rachel moved like a zombie as Jasmine led her back to her seat. She actually had to help the girl sit down—but that was wonderful because Jasmine knew the women were watching and she demonstrated her compassion for the poor, stupid child.

Then Jasmine took her place, folded her hands in her lap, and turned to Cecelia King as if the woman was about to give the most important speech in the world.

Chapter TWELVE

Uggghhhhh!!!!" Rachel screamed as she threw the hotel's lamp against the wall.

"Have you lost your mind?" Lester screamed.

Rachel stopped mid-rant. She didn't know how long she'd been in the hotel suite, but judging by the broken lamp, the overturned coffee table, and the way Nia was cowering in the corner, it had been long enough to terrify her children.

Her son was standing behind Lester in the doorway, looking scared out of his mind. He must've run outside and called Lester when she came stomping into the suite like a stark raving lunatic.

Lester's admonishment and the silent tears trickling down Nia's face brought her back to reality. She hadn't had an angry explosion like that in years. Rachel closed her eyes and inhaled. *How in the world had she let that woman push her to this point?*

"I . . . I'm sorry, kids," Rachel said, her eyes watering. "Mommy didn't mean to scare you. I was just really mad."

"But when I got mad and broke Jordan's airplane, you said no matter how mad you get, you shouldn't break other people's things," Nia softly replied.

"And you shouldn't," Rachel responded, walking over and pulling her daughter out of the corner. "Mommy did a very bad thing, but she's going to use her own money to pay for the lamp."

"Like you made me use my allowance to pay for Jordan's plane?" Nia asked.

Rachel nodded. "I'm sorry I scared you." She looked up at Jordan. "You, too, Jordan."

He looked relieved that she wasn't mad about him going to get Lester.

"Why don't you take your sister down to the gift shop and buy her some ice cream." She pulled a twenty out of her purse and handed it to her son. "Keep the change."

"For real?" Jordan exclaimed. If anything could make Jordan forget about problems, it was money.

"For real."

"What about me?" Nia said.

Rachel reached in her purse and pulled out two five-dollar bills.

"Yay!" Nia said. She waved the money in her brother's face. "I got more than you. I got more than you."

"No, you don't."

"Unh-huh. You only have one bill. I got two," she sang.

"You are such a dumb dork," he said as he walked toward the door.

"Jordan, don't talk to your sister like that," Lester said, before moving to let them pass.

Lester let the sounds of their arguing fade before he stepped inside and closed the door.

"Do you want to tell me what's going on?"

"It's that bi—that witch, Jasmine," Rachel said, her anger returning. "You will not believe what she did at the luncheon."

Rachel paced back and forth as she relayed the whole sordid story. After Jasmine swooped in with her fake Wonder Woman cape, the whole atmosphere had shifted. Cecelia had barely said two words to her the rest of the luncheon. Some of the women even spent the whole time throwing her dirty looks. Rachel had tried to apologize afterward, even telling Cecelia that someone had switched out her bio. Cecelia had barely listened to her apology, and quickly made her exit. Rachel didn't know how, but she knew exactly *who* that someone had been.

"Rachel, I'm sure it wasn't as bad as you're making it out to be." Lester motioned around the room. "It surely didn't warrant this."

"Are you freakin' kidding me? It was worse than bad, it was horrendous. And what if it costs you the election?"

"Then it wasn't God's will for me to win," Lester said, walking over to begin picking up the broken pieces of the lamp. "I just thank God the babies weren't in here. Jordan said they were with your dad and Brenda."

"Do you hear yourself?" Rachel screamed. "This is not something to be taken lightly. This tramp is trying to sabotage everything we worked for."

Lester released a frustrated sigh. "First of all, I doubt it's that serious." He turned and looked Rachel in the eye. "And if this election is going to turn you into this crazed woman, I will just withdraw from the race."

"You'll do no such thing." She knew there was no way Lester was going to play dirty. But *she* wasn't above it at all. In fact, she had just the dirt she needed. Her trump card. She hadn't planned to stoop this low, but the game had changed. That old freak had proven she could *and would* play dirty. But Jasmine didn't know dirty and Rachel was definitely about to show it to her.

"I'm going to tell the front desk that we have a lamp to pay for," Lester said, dumping the last of the shattered ceramic into the trash. "Then, I'm going back to the budget meeting. The public praise and worship session starts in four hours and I'd like to get some rest."

Rachel didn't reply as her husband walked out. She didn't have time to be concerned with him. Four hours was just enough time to put her plan into action.

Rachel couldn't help but notice how Jasmine kept staring at her throughout the worship service. She was probably wondering why Rachel was smiling, seemingly carefree as she got caught up in the praise and worship. But Rachel was focused, her eye was on the prize, and she was ready for her plan to be unveiled— right in front of this packed ballroom.

When she had found out this little tidbit, she'd filed it away because it was a little too much, even for her. She knew what she was about to do would really make Lester mad. But he'd just have to get over it because there was no way Rachel was about to let that tramp get away with what she did at the luncheon.

"Can I get an amen?" Reverend King said as the music took on a softer tone.

Amens reverberated throughout the ballroom.

"After that powerful message from this evening's guest preacher, Rev. Payne, I know there's some soul that feels the need to come to Jesus."

Yes! Rachel silently proclaimed.

"I know there are a lot of saints in the house, but if there are any sinners among us who long to know God, come, come now and share your testimony," Reverend King said.

A couple of people made their way up front. Rachel's smile spread as the third person stood. She looked exactly like Rachel expected her to. The long, platinum blond wig. The leopard-print spandex pants. The black crop tank that was cut too high at the bottom and too low at the top. And the makeup. Whew. The bright blue glitter eye shadow was overpowering and it looked like she'd used ruby red lipstick on her lips *and* her cheeks. She had to be pushing forty, but years of hard living made her look a lot older. Rachel couldn't have picked a better representative if she had created her herself.

Rachel waited anxiously as the first two people gave their testimony. She wasn't even sure what they had said. All of her attention was focused—like most people in the room—on the harlot standing at the end, smacking on a wad of gum like it was the last piece on earth.

Rachel sneaked a look over at Jasmine, who was sitting across the aisle with her husband. Jasmine looked like she'd seen a ghost and Rachel knew instantly that her source had been right on the money. She actually was grateful Jacqueline wasn't here. It would be a shame for the little girl to witness what was about to go down.

"Hey, e'rebody," the woman said after Reverend King handed

her the mic. "First of all, givin' honor to God and all that stuff. My name is Alize. Well, my real name is LaQuanta, but e'rebody call me Alize. Thank you for lettin' me say my piece. I just happened to be here in the hotel meeting a . . . a . . . umm, a customer." She paused and released a giggle. "But don't worry, it wasn't nobody from y'all's convention," she said to a few nervous chuckles. "Anyway, I was waiting on him, when I spotted somebody I knew from back in the day." How she continued to chew her gum and talk was beyond Rachel, but it just added to the outrageousness of it all.

"Anyway," she continued, "I couldn't get close enough to her to say hi, so I followed her in here to try and talk to her because I used to really look up to her back in the day when we was stripping together."

Gasps filled the room. It took everything in her power for Rachel not to look over at Jasmine and burst out laughing.

"Anyway, she was always one of the classy strippers down at Foxtails. And even when we used to, um, give private lessons, she was still one of them high-class h—"

"Yeah, okay," Reverend King said, snatching the mic away.

The woman snatched the mic right back. "I ain't done. You said you wanted to hear from people that had a testimony. Well, ain't nobody been tested like me!" She scanned the crowd until her eyes settled on Jasmine. "And if Pepper Pulaski, oh, my bad, I guess you don't go by that anymore. If Jasmine Cox can pull herself up and be all up in here with all you sidity folks, then maybe I can, too. Thank you, Jazzy, for showing me that I don't have to keep turning tricks and showing my body. I'm gettin' too old anyway. I need a new come-up, so I wanna be like you and do this church thang. You my she-ro, girl. Call me. I'm still at Foxtails, although I just mostly do private stuff and bartending now cuz I can't shake it like I used to." She did a little wiggle. "So drop by before you leave LA. We moved, though. We on Crenshaw now. Most of the girls are gone, but Buck is still there. He'd love to see you, so come by tonight. And bring the bishop," she said, blowing Hosea a kiss.

Every eye in the room turned to Jasmine, including a horrified Cecelia King. Rachel tried her best to look surprised as well, but this was so absolutely perfect that she couldn't contain her joy. Lester eyed Rachel suspiciously, but she'd already planned to lie, deny, and lie some more. This actually hadn't even been something Rachel had discovered. This was divine intervention. Some hoochie-looking lady had walked up to her in the lobby yesterday and handed her an envelope with all the info on Jasmine's stripper past. When Rachel had eyed her with skepticism, the woman had used Rachel's phone (she said she didn't want to be linked to anything) and called this Alize.

At first, Alize had been hesitant because she said it had been so long ago that she barely remembered Jasmine. But the three hundred bucks Rachel offered helped to refresh her memory. Suddenly, she recalled how "uppity Jasmine Cox was" and how she always "thought she was better than everybody else," and she said it would be her pleasure to "help put Jasmine on blast."

Rachel hadn't planned to use the information, as juicy as it was, but then Jasmine had pulled that stunt this morning and the game changed. So Rachel called Alize back, offered her another five hundred to come over to the hotel tonight, and Alize had been all too willing.

"Okay, so am I saved now?" Alize asked, turning her attention back to Reverend King.

"Umm, I'm sorry, little lady. It, um, it isn't that easy," he stammered.

"Awww, hell. Guess it's gonna have to wait until another time. I gotta private party with some rappers in an hour and until the Good Lord put some Benjamins in my pocket, I'm gon' have to keep doin' what I do. But y'all pray for me. I feel an anointin' coming on. Hallelujah!" she sang as she strutted down the center aisle and out the door.

Chapter
THIRTEEN

"Shame" and "sorry" were two words that were foreign to Jasmine; they'd never had any place in any part of her psyche. She'd never been ashamed—not of the millions of lies that she'd told, not of the humiliation she'd bestowed upon her first husband, not even of all the heartache she'd caused for the women whose husbands she'd bedded over the years.

No, there'd never been room for shame because she'd always had a reason. And her days as a stripper? Please! That was when she had the greatest reason of all. Without that pole, she would've never graduated from college.

So never any shame, never any reason to be sorry.

But now, as she held Hosea's hand and stepped down the aisle of the convention center, her head was high, though she moved humbly . . . with shame. Not that she was sorry for what she'd done; it was just that she'd been caught . . . and so publicly . . . and at the worst possible time.

She'd prayed last night that this revelation wouldn't cost Hosea this election. But already, she was sure that God hadn't been listening to her. The arena was packed. There were more people here this morning than at the worship service last night. All to see her, no doubt. All to hear what Hosea was going to say.

As she approached the front, Jasmine caught sight of Lester and Rachel holding court at the edge of the platform that had been set up as an altar.

That skank Rachel.

There was not a single doubt in Jasmine's mind—Rachel Adams was behind this. Jasmine's eyes stayed on the woman, glaring, willing Rachel to turn and face her.

As if she felt Jasmine's glare, Rachel turned around.

At first, Rachel wore a smile, a grin really, her face shining with the delight of triumph. But as her eyes remained locked with Jasmine's, her smile faded slightly, became just a smirk, then vanished. Right there, Rachel seemed to shrink before Jasmine's eyes. Oh, yeah, Rachel still held her head up and stuck her chin out. But Jasmine could almost see the woman's heart beating through the cheap fake silk blouse that looked like it had been purchased at a swap meet several years ago.

Good! Jasmine thought, feeling just a bit of satisfaction at Rachel's fear. It was clear that the Adams girl had done her homework, but she hadn't delved deep enough. Because if she had, she would've known that Jasmine Cox Larson Bush was not the one to be messed with.

Rachel was going to pay; Jasmine had decided it was time to finally implement the big plan that Mae Frances had been talking to her about.

But first, she had to get through this session.

At the front, Lester shook Hosea's hands and the two men exchanged a greeting that Jasmine didn't hear. But she didn't say a word. Just kept her glare on Rachel, instilling more fear until the trick lowered her eyes.

At least Rachel wasn't totally dumb. At least she was smart enough to be afraid.

Jasmine took her seat, the same one she'd been sitting in last night when the stripper had called her out. She didn't have to turn around to see the stares; she could feel them. If she wasn't trying to get her husband elected, she would've stood up at the altar and told every single last one of them to go to hell.

But that was not how a proper first lady behaved.

She would just have to endure it. If this went down the way they had planned, in an hour she would be back in all of their good graces. The men had decided how to handle this situation.

It was not the way she would've handled it; but since she was the problem, she didn't have a big voice in what was to be the solution.

At least they had a plan, one that she prayed was going to work. One that they'd come up with last night after they left the arena . . .

Never had hundreds of black people been in one place, sitting together in such absolute silence. But that was what filled the convention center as Alize handed the microphone back to Reverend King and then sauntered up the aisle, swaying her hips as if she was naked on a stage right now. The hundreds had been stunned, never taking their eyes away from Alize, not until she sashayed right out of the door.

Jasmine had been the most shocked of all. Had Alize been a stripper with her twenty years ago? Really? And she was *still* at Foxtails? Really?

If that was true, that woman needed to be arrested—not because she was too young, but because she was way too old. There had to be a law against anyone who was closer to fifty than to forty taking off their clothes and scaring people like that.

She had wanted to run after that heffa, call her out, call her a liar, and demand that Alize restore her good name in front of these women and their husbands, whom she'd worked so hard to get on her side.

But as the silence broke and the arena filled with shocked chatter, Hosea had pulled her to follow Pastor Griffith as he led Hosea, Jasmine, and the rest of their entourage through the side door.

"There was no reason for us to leave," Hosea protested, though he quickly followed behind his father and Pastor Griffith. "That's not how I operate. I stand up and face the enemy."

"I appreciate that, but we need to regroup," Pastor Griffith said, taking a quick look at Jasmine. "This election is too important to make the next move without thinking it all the way through."

Back at the hotel, Pastor Griffith had given instructions to

"I got it," Pastor Griffith said. "I'll rush back in the session, pretending that the emergency call I just got was about Rachel. I'll stand up, tell them that that's why Lester Adams had to leave in such a hurry and I'll make a plea for us to have a special offering to raise money for Rachel's bond so that we can get her out of jail."

"That's perfect!" Mae Frances said.

"I'll paint a picture," he said. "A whole story about how they found the bracelet, and the police coming and Cecelia being right there when they handcuffed Rachel and dragged her away."

Mae Frances beamed at him as if she was proud. Jasmine just continued staring and thinking.

"The only thing," Pastor Griffith said to Jasmine, "is I don't want you here; I don't want you in the hotel. I don't want anyone to be able to call your room or to see you anywhere in the hotel—at least not for the next few hours."

"Why not?"

"Because I want Cecelia hounded by these people. I want people calling her, I want people knocking on their door, I want people texting her. I want the Kings so overwhelmed that they will never again have anything to do with the Adams family! So, I don't want you anywhere to be found to answer questions."

"That's not going to work. Hosea is going to call me as soon as he hears about this. He knows I was with Cecelia and Rachel."

"I'll tell Hosea that since your children are hanging out at all the kids' events today, you knew they were safe and you wanted to get Mae Frances away from this craziness. Don't worry, Hosea will probably call you, but I'll take care of your husband. I've got him under control."

Jasmine and Mae Frances spoke at the same time. "What does that mean?"

He looked at Jasmine, then turned to face Mae Frances. "Don't get testy, ladies. I simply mean that I have the situation— the whole situation—under control."

"That's not what you said," Jasmine stated.

"Well, that's what I meant." The pastor stared at Jasmine as if he dared her to challenge him any more.

The women glanced at each other, but when Pastor Griffith picked his wallet from his pocket and tossed five one-hundred-dollar bills to Mae Frances, she seemed to forget his ominous words.

But the money didn't distract Jasmine. "What's that for?" she asked.

"You two go out."

"Where?" The questions all came from Jasmine; Mae Frances no longer had any concerns. She'd already scooped that money up as if it was a million dollars. "And for how long?" Jasmine kept the questions coming.

"Just a couple of hours. Go back to the mall, finish up your shopping. Go out to eat; all this work has got to have made you hungry." He had tucked his wallet away, but he opened it up again and passed five bills to Jasmine.

She stared at the money, then shook her head. "I'm fine." Looking him straight in the eyes, she said, "I don't need your money."

He chuckled. "Sweetheart, this is not about needs, it's all about wants. And because you and I want the same thing—for your husband to be the president of the Coalition—you *need* to take this money, and let me do my thing."

She stared at the five hundred dollars for a little while longer; and again, she wanted to ask him, what was in it for him? But after a few moments, her fingers slowly curled around the money.

He smiled.

Mae Frances laughed and said, "Let's go, Jasmine Larson."

It took her a moment to gather herself, but with a final glance at Pastor Griffith, Jasmine lifted her bags and followed Mae Frances out of the restaurant.

Chapter TWENTY

The eight hours had felt like an eternity. But Rachel was just grateful to be out of that hellhole. Her idea to call Melinda had been right on the money. Melinda had marched over to the Beverly Center, flashed her ID, and asked that security guard to retell his story on camera. Naturally, he'd spouted some mess about the company's privacy policy, but when Melinda had demanded to see the surveillance tape, and it showed Rachel just standing around looking irritated and not blatantly stealing as he'd claimed, he'd stuttered, backtracked, and said maybe he'd been mistaken. Rachel had hoped the tape would've shown Jasmine setting her up, but Melinda said it only showed Jasmine's back to the camera and there was no way to prove she'd done anything.

That had been frustrating, but at least the flustered guard had decided he didn't want to go on camera lying about her. He never admitted to anything, but the manager had told Melinda they didn't want the "negative press," so they wouldn't be pressing charges.

Rachel had decided she, however, would be filing charges. Or a lawsuit. Or something for false arrest, false imprisonment, lying on a customer, anything she could make stick.

But right now, she had a bigger fish to fry. While she'd sat in that jail cell, she'd been consumed with thoughts of how to make Jasmine pay. But nothing she could think of was punishment enough.

"Are you okay? You're so quiet," Lester said, snapping Rachel out of her vengeful thoughts.

"I'm just happy to be out of that place." She leaned back in the car seat. Lester had been waiting with a driver when she'd walked out and she'd been so happy that he'd had the good sense to get a luxury Town Car. She sank down in the plush leather seats. "Where are the kids? Do they know what's going on?" she asked.

"No. Brooklyn and Lewis are with Brenda and your dad. Nia and Jordan are at the kids' coalition slumber party tonight. The only person that knows anything to my knowledge is Deacon Tisdale. I had to tell him so he could work on getting me the money for the bail."

Rachel sighed. At least Deacon Tisdale, the treasurer of their church, was discreet. "What about everyone else? I'm sure Jasmine couldn't wait to get back and blab to everyone at the hotel what happened."

"Actually, no one has said a word about it other than Mrs. King. When I was leaving to come pick you up, she asked me for an update."

"I hope you explained to her that they'd dropped the charges."

"I did and I told her how you'd never stolen anything in your life. She looked a little skeptical but relieved."

Rachel glanced out the window of the moving car. She'd made such progress with Cecelia this week. Even though the charges had been dropped, Rachel was sure the whole experience had left a sour taste in Cecelia's mouth.

Yet another reason for her to hate Jasmine.

The driver pulled up to the hotel. Rachel was grateful that the lobby was fairly empty. Lester said no one really knew but she didn't trust that for a minute. She was positive Jasmine had told anyone who passed about what happened. So Rachel just needed tonight to regroup, get her head together, and prepare for tomorrow's formal nominating meeting. She probably would need to address this whole matter. It was an issue she decided to bring up with Lester later.

Rachel had just made it to the elevator when one of the men who had been with the Bush entourage came rushing toward her.

"Rachel! Are you okay?"

Rachel raised an eyebrow at this old man and his fake concern.

"Excuse me?" she said, cutting her eyes at Lester.

"How are you, Pastor Griffith?" Lester said, stepping in.

The man took Rachel's hand. "Oh, don't worry about me. We need to be concerned about Rachel. I imagine it was horrific having to spend the afternoon in jail!" His voice was loud and carried across the corridor, causing a few people to stop and stare their way.

Rachel had to take small, deep breaths to keep from losing it. She didn't know this Pastor Griffith, but she did know he was on the Bushes' side, so his concern about her was a big act and she was about to tell him about himself.

She snatched her hand away. "You know—"

"Pastor Griffith"—Lester must have known Rachel was about to go off, because he stepped in, cutting her off—"thank you for your concern, but Rachel is fine. It was all a big misunderstanding."

Pastor Griffith shook his head. "I heard they found a nine-hundred-dollar diamond bracelet in her bag."

"Again, it was all a misunderstanding," Lester said.

"I just hate that for you. I am sure that was so traumatic for you," Pastor Griffith said, his voice still raised, "to be carted out of a mall in handcuffs, then just thrown into jail!" *Were his eyes actually watering up?*

"You don't need to be concerned about me," Rachel said as calmly as she could. She glanced over to the people who were blatantly staring her way. "Someone tried to set me up. The police figured that out, which is why they let me go."

"Well, that is fantastic news because I would hate for you to have spent the night in jail." He was a great actor, because he looked like he was really worried about Rachel. Luckily, she could smell a con artist a mile away and Pastor Griffith definitely bore the stench of someone who was up to no good.

"Again, thank you, Pastor Griffith, but as you can imagine,

my wife wants to go get some rest," Lester said, stepping to Rachel's side.

"Well, you just let me know if there's anything I can do," Pastor Griffith said.

"Like that would ever happen," Rachel muttered.

"Pardon me?" Pastor Griffith said.

"Nothing," Lester quickly interjected. "Come on, sweetheart. I know you just want to go upstairs and lie down." He led her on to the elevator.

"Can you believe the nerve of that man," Rachel said as she watched Pastor Griffith wave from across the lobby. "He knows doggone well he could care less about me being arrested. Everybody knows he's pushing for Rev. Bush, so why he's trying to fake the funk is beyond me." Rachel was pissed, but after the day she'd had, she couldn't waste any more energy on this Pastor Griffith.

"So, are you going to get some rest?" Lester asked as the elevator door closed.

"Actually, I want to see my kids."

Lester pushed the button for their floor. "Well, Brooklyn and Lewis are asleep, and you know if you wake them up, it's going to be brutal trying to get them back down."

She nodded. He was right about that. "Well, at least let me see Nia and Jordan."

"They're at the slumber party," Lester said.

"Okay, but I still want to stop in and see them, say good night at least."

Lester punched the button to the twelfth floor as the elevator rose. "Okay. They're in 1202. It's the suite at the end of the hall. Do you need me to go with you?"

"No, I'm fine. You go on up."

"Actually, I need to run by Deacon Tisdale's room and update him on everything." He handed her the room key. "Here's the extra key. I'll just see you back in the room."

"That's fine," Rachel said as the elevator doors opened on the twelfth floor. She stepped out and looked down the hall to room

1202. The sounds of squealing children reverberated through the door. She knocked several times but the kids were so loud they couldn't hear, so no one answered.

Rachel was just about to turn and leave when the door swung open. Her son Jordan and another little boy stood in the doorway.

"Ma?" Jordan said. "What are you doing here?"

"Hey, honey. I just came to check on you."

"Awww, Ma, why you checking on me?"

"I just wanted to come hug you good night."

Jordan looked mortified as the little boy next to him started snickering. Rachel shook her head, not about to get into it with her son. "Is Nia in there?"

"Yeah, all the girls are in one room. She's been whining for you since we got here."

That warmed Rachel's heart. "Can you go get her?"

Jordan seemed all too happy to dart off. The other boy was quickly on his heels. Rachel stood with her foot propping the door open. She would've gone in, but all that noise was making her head hurt.

A few minutes later, the door swung back open and Nia bounced into her mother's arms. "Mommy!" she said.

"Hey, baby," Rachel said, hugging her daughter tightly. She was just about to say something else when she looked up to see who had just stepped out the door and was standing behind Nia. "Hi, Jacqueline," Rachel said slowly.

"Jacquie's my friend now," Nia said excitedly as she took Jacqueline's hand. "She's not mad at me anymore for messing up her dress."

"Well, that's wonderful. Are you girls having a good time?"

"The boys are being mean," Nia said. "They put them in another room, but they're still picking on us. Can I come with you?"

Rachel smiled. She was tired and really had wanted to just hug her daughter and keep moving. But how could she turn down such a sweet request?

"Okay, honey. We can pop some popcorn and watch a movie."

"Oooohhh." Nia stopped and looked over at Jacqueline. "Can Jacqueline come, too?"

Rachel's heart stopped as an idea for the perfect payback sprouted in her mind. But this was a low blow. Considering the horror Jasmine had gone through the last time Jacqueline came up missing, Rachel couldn't do that to her again.

"Ummm, well . . ." Rachel began.

"Please? I wanna come," Jacqueline said. "The boys are being mean to me, too. Can I come? Pretty please?"

She couldn't inflict that type of pain on another mother. But then Rachel thought back over the last ten hours. She thought back over the humiliation of being arrested, of sitting in that jail cell, of Cecelia's disgust. When she processed all of that, she found herself saying, "That sounds like a great idea. You can spend the night with us. We'll cut off the phone so nobody can disturb us and just have our own private slumber party. You can go back to your room in the morning." A sick feeling rose in her gut, but Rachel shook it off as she took both girls' hands and led them to the elevator. "I'll call the chaperones when we get to the room and tell them that you're spending the night with me."

Chapter
TWENTY-ONE

From the moment that Jasmine had married a man of such means, shopping had been her third love—behind Hosea and her children. But she found no love in her favorite habit today.

In fact, she felt like she'd been exiled to some kind of shopping prison and Mae Frances was her prison guard.

She and Mae Frances hadn't returned to the Beverly Center. Instead, Mae Frances had dragged her to Rodeo Drive, where Jasmine told her that the five hundred dollars that Pastor Griffith had given her would do nothing more than buy a good meal and some wine. But Mae Frances had insisted, and as the April breeze swept through Beverly Hills, they sauntered up and down the famed streets known for the designer stores and haute couture fashion. Mae Frances squealed like a tourist when she walked past Harry Winston and Chanel and Hermès and David Yurman, although Jasmine didn't know why. Mae Frances lived on the Upper East Side of Manhattan—she'd definitely seen these stores before.

Maybe it was just the California air. Or maybe she was still excited that they had pulled off such a scheme, and Rachel Adams now sat in jail not too many blocks away from where they shopped. Whatever it was that had Mae Frances smiling and figuring out how she was going to spend her money, it had Jasmine brooding.

"You need to get it together, Jasmine Larson," Mae Frances had said to her once. But after that warning, Mae Frances had ignored her friend, and focused just on the stores.

Even when Jasmine decided that they should go to Crustacean for dinner, and Mae Frances had marveled at that famous walk-on-water entrance, Jasmine's mood had not changed.

"What has your panties in a bunch?" Mae Frances asked right after they'd both ordered the charbroiled colossal tiger shrimp from the Special Kitchen. "Don't tell me that you're still thinking about Rachel? There's no need to worry about her."

"No, it's not her," Jasmine said, though she wasn't sure if her words were totally true. She didn't really know if it was Rachel or what that had her stomach churning—like something bad was brewing.

"How well do you know Pastor Griffith?"

Mae Frances frowned as if she didn't understand the question. "I can't even count the years," she said. Jasmine wondered if she was purposely being evasive.

But she didn't ask any more questions. When an hour had passed, and Mae Frances texted Pastor Griffith, Jasmine held her breath.

"Great!" Mae Frances said as she looked down at her phone. "He said it's safe to come back." Then she laughed. "He added that the Kings have had enough. We need to celebrate, Jasmine Larson. With another glass of wine."

"We need to get back to the hotel," Jasmine said, signaling the waiter for the bill. "I want to see my children."

When they jumped in the cab to head back downtown, Jasmine offered the driver twenty dollars over the meter to get them to the hotel in fifteen minutes. It took him twenty-two minutes and she'd tipped him a twenty (from Pastor Griffith's money) anyway, just because she was so glad to be back.

And she was even happier when Hosea met her at the hotel's entrance.

"Babe!" she said, dropping her bags and wrapping her arms around him.

"Whoa!" Hosea chuckled. "I should send you out shopping more often."

She said, "It's just been a long day . . . and I missed you."

"Well, I don't know how you had time to miss me when you were in the middle of all the excitement today."

Jasmine glanced at Mae Frances before she said, "I know. Rachel arrested for shoplifting. Isn't that something?"

"It was, but thank God it was all cleared up."

The women spoke together. "What are you talking about?"

"Turns out the security guard at the store you guys were in retracted. Said he didn't see what he thought he saw, and the tapes in the store didn't show anything." He leaned over and whispered to Jasmine, "I have to admit, darlin', for a moment I thought you had something to do with it. But the tapes didn't show anything except for three ladies out doing their thing."

"So, how did the bracelet get in her bag?" Mae Frances asked.

Hosea shrugged as he took the shopping bags from his wife and Mae Frances. "No idea. I'm just glad that it's all cleared up now, though for a while this afternoon, Reverend King and his wife were quite upset. People were almost attacking Lady Cecelia with all of their questions."

Jasmine glanced at Mae Frances and she was sure that her friend's thoughts were the same as hers—at least that part of the plan had worked.

"Well, all I want to do is go to the children's suite, hug them, then go up to ours and crawl right into bed."

"Mind if I join you?"

"You better! Are you finished for the night?"

He nodded. "I think they know they kept the men away from their wives long enough. Plus, they want us well rested for the nominating session tomorrow."

Hours had passed since the last time Jasmine smiled. At least this whole process, this whole week, was coming to an end. Tomorrow, Hosea would officially be nominated, and then two days after that . . . it would be over. No more tricks from that trick. And, she wouldn't have to deal with Pastor Griffith anymore either. Jasmine didn't like mistrusting him, especially when he'd done nothing except help them. But there were too many things that made her uneasy and she just wanted to get away from all of these people.

Inside the elevator, Hosea said, "Oh, I forgot to tell you, darlin', Jacqueline is at the Coalition slumber party."

"What?"

"The slumber party, remember? She's been asking to go to that all week."

As the doors parted on the fifth floor, Jasmine asked, "So, Mrs. Sloss is with her, right?"

"No, she stayed behind in the suite with Zaya."

The three had been moving together, but Jasmine stopped in the middle of the hallway. "So . . . who's with Jacquie?"

Hosea put his hand on her shoulder, and said, "She's at the party with five chaperones. I dropped her off and checked out things myself. She'll be fine." He paused. "She's safe."

Jasmine turned around, marched back to the elevator.

"Where are you going?" Hosea asked.

"To get Jacquie."

"No, Jasmine." Hosea gently tugged her hand, pulling her in the direction of the suite. "She wanted to go to the party and we have to start letting her be a little more independent. She's begging for that and she needs it. And here in this hotel, at this convention, is a wonderful and safe place for us to start."

She took a deep breath, then followed Hosea back down the hall toward the suite where Mrs. Sloss and Mae Frances were staying with Zaya. "I just want you to know that I'm going to hug Zaya and then we're going to get Jacquie." The look on Hosea's face made her say, "Okay, we won't get her, but I want to at least give her a hug."

Mrs. Sloss greeted them with the news that Zaya was already asleep. Jasmine tiptoed into the bedroom, with Hosea behind her, and together they stood above the bed, watching their three-year-old sleep.

Hosea put his arms around Jasmine and held her close. "Our

children are fine," he whispered. "Our children are safe. You know that no matter what, I will always see to that."

Jasmine knew that was the truth—there was a castrated man in prison in New York who had dared to mess with their daughter. In her heart, Jasmine knew that her children were safe, especially here. But still, it was hard to let go of Jacquie, when she had such trouble letting go of the memories of that horrible time.

She kissed Zaya's cheek, and without looking away, she said, "That's all I want to do with Jacquie. Just kiss her good night."

"I already did that for the both of us," Hosea said. "If we go to the room now, we'll disrupt the fun and she'll probably want to leave with us. She has our numbers if anything happens. If she wants to call . . . if she wants to leave."

Jasmine shook her head, so unsure.

"We have to begin to trust again," he whispered. "Trust ourselves, trust Jacquie, trust God."

Jasmine leaned over and kissed their son again, then with everything that was inside of her, she let Hosea lead her to their hotel suite without stopping for Jacqueline.

They stepped inside their room, but never made it to the bedroom. Before the door was closed, Hosea had Jasmine in his arms. His kisses were as gentle as his touch and she remembered why she loved this man, in every way . . . this gentle man.

He slipped off her jacket; then the camisole that she wore underneath. His lips followed his fingers, his cool tongue setting every inch of her body—even the parts that he hadn't gotten to yet—on fire. When she reached for him, he held her hands away, letting her know that he was in control tonight.

On the living room couch, they made love for the first time since they'd arrived in Los Angeles; their kisses, and touches, and moans let the other know how much they'd been missed.

And then they took their love salsa into the bedroom, where they united again and again for more hours, until there was no more room for their pleasure.

Exhausted, they lay in each other's arms. In just minutes, Jasmine heard the rhythm of Hosea's sleep breathing. But though she was satisfied and wanted nothing more than to rest inside her husband's arms, she could not.

What was this disconcerting feeling that boiled inside her? Was it all because of what she'd done to Rachel? It couldn't be that. Rachel was out, and wasn't even going to be charged. So why was she so concerned about her?

Jasmine closed her eyes, but still she couldn't sleep. So she just lay in Hosea's arms and waited. Waited for morning to come.

Chapter
TWENTY-TWO

Morning came, though it hadn't come fast enough. Jasmine was out of the shower before the alarm rang at six.

Hosea rolled over and slapped the clock. His eyes were still filled with sleep when he peered at Jasmine pinning up her hair in front of the mirror.

"Where are you going? Running?" he asked, eyeing her jogging suit.

"I'm going to get Jacquie."

He glanced at the clock as if he'd forgotten that he just turned the alarm off. "Darlin', they are not even awake yet."

"That's okay. I was thinking about bringing the children up here for breakfast. We haven't spent enough time with them."

Hosea plopped back down onto the bed. "Can't we do that in an hour or two? We don't have to be in the hall until noon."

Pushing the last hairpin in place, Jasmine turned to her husband. "Of course. I'll just hang out with the kids in their suite, and then we'll come up here about seven thirty or eight."

When she leaned over to kiss him, he grabbed her. "The point of waiting a couple of hours for the kids is so that I can have more time with my beautiful wife. What do I have to do to talk you into coming back into bed with me?"

She pressed her lips against his as her fingers tickled his naked torso. "Tonight. We'll celebrate after the nomination." Another kiss, and then she was gone.

It had felt like a week had passed since she'd last seen Jacqueline. Jasmine knew it was way too early for her not-a-morning-child daughter, but it didn't matter. She needed to lay her eyes on Jacqueline, and then after that, they'd spend some quality time as a family.

She didn't even bother to wait for the elevator; it was just a few flights down. It took several rounds of knocking before she even heard the first sounds of someone stirring on the other side of the door.

"Who is it?" a woman mumbled through the closed door.

"Jasmine Bush."

Jasmine heard the lock click, then the door opened slowly to reveal a short, thick, young woman wearing an oversize American Baptist Convention T-shirt and leggings. "I'm here to pick up Jacqueline Bush."

With her fist, the girl wiped her eye. "None of the kids are up yet." She yawned.

Jasmine folded her arms; her expression and her stance asked her question—what does that have to do with anything? Aloud, she said, "That's okay, I'll wake up my daughter."

When the girl sighed as if Jasmine was intruding, Jasmine wanted to ask where *her* mother was, but she stepped inside, and saw bodies everywhere . . . on the couch, on the floor, in the chairs.

"These are all the boys." The girl yawned again as she led Jasmine through the maze of kids. "Some of the chaperones are in there." She pointed to one side of the suite. "And the girls are in this room."

She opened the door and Jasmine was once again faced with bodies. Tall ones, short ones, under covers, in sleeping bags— about twenty altogether.

It was Jasmine's turn to sigh. Wasn't a mother supposed to know her children anywhere, anytime? It would have been easier to just call out her name, but it really was early, and these kids had probably been up until just a few hours ago.

So, she stepped over the bodies, stopping at each one, absolutely sure that the next one would be her darling daughter.

And then Jasmine got to the end of the room.

She felt her heart begin to race, but she took a deep breath and calmed herself. She turned to the girl. "Where's Jacquie?"

The girl shrugged. "I didn't really get to know all their names."

"What do you mean?" Jasmine asked, her voice rising as she stepped through the sleeping bags once again.

"We just let the kids play and hang out. We didn't ask their names."

The panic attacked like a lion. "Jacquie!" Jasmine yelled out. Now she ripped the sleeping bags from the girls, waking each one up in the process. "Oh, my God! Jacquie! Jacquie!"

It was exactly the way it was before. Searching, calling for her daughter . . . and no answer.

"Jacquie," she screamed, waking up everyone in the suite.

The chaperones dashed into the room.

"What's going on?" a gray-haired woman asked.

"Where's my daughter?" Jasmine cried. "My husband, Pastor Bush, brought her here last night and now she's gone." She tore through the girls again; most were standing up now. Then she raced into the bathroom before she rushed into the living room, waking all the boys.

"Jacquie!" she screamed. "Jacquie!" she cried.

"Mrs. Bush, Mrs. Bush, calm down," the older woman said to her.

Jasmine whipped around and had to fight hard to keep her hands from closing around the woman's neck. "Calm down? Someone has taken my daughter!"

Two of the chaperones were on cell phones, and as Jasmine rushed to the other side of the suite, she yelled out to no one in particular, "Call my husband!"

Not many minutes passed before Hosea burst into the room, and Jasmine was still searching—under the beds, behind the sofas, in the closets.

"Jasmine!"

She wanted to rush to him for comfort, but it was his fault that they were back in this place. "She's gone!" Jasmine cried.

"You left her here and now she's gone!" Her intent was to beat his chest until he hurt as much as she already did. But when he pulled her close, she fell into his arms.

"We'll find her," he said. "I'll find her."

"My baby's gone again." She trembled in his arms. "My baby's gone again."

Three men from hotel security entered the room and Hosea told them how he'd dropped off their daughter last night for the slumber party.

"Would anyone else have picked her up?"

"No!" Jasmine cried. "Her nanny is in their suite with her grandmother, and her grandfather is probably still asleep." She crumbled in Hosea's arms. "Oh, my God. It can't happen again. Please, God! It can't be happening again."

Hosea helped Jasmine to her feet, then settled her onto the couch. But though he wanted to rush through the suite himself, he couldn't leave Jasmine—she would never survive without him by her side.

As he held Jasmine, he asked one of the security guards to call his father and Mae Frances. And while the other guards questioned the children, before they were escorted back to their parents, Hosea held Jasmine in his arms and fought his own tears.

This could not possibly be happening again.

Within minutes, they were joined by more security and hotel personnel. Then Reverend Bush, Pastor Griffith, and Reverend Penn and his wife rushed in.

"Lady Jasmine," Coco Penn called. "Is there anything I can do?"

Jasmine didn't respond. She didn't move at all; she couldn't.

And then Mae Frances came in. Without saying a word, she took Hosea's place, and now Jasmine rested in her arms.

"The police have been called," the visibly shaken hotel manager told them. "They'll be here in a few minutes."

"And I've informed Reverend King," Pastor Griffith said. "Mrs. King said that she'll be right down."

Jasmine closed her eyes, now wanting the sleep that had

eluded her last night. She would only survive through unconsciousness . . . because she was never going to live a day without her daughter. If Jacqueline was missing again, she would go, too. She'd much prefer to die than to live with the pain of another day without her child.

As the hotel suite came alive around her, Jasmine wondered what the end of this day would bring. Would Jacquie be back or would Hosea have to shoot someone else?

"Jasmine!"

Not even the voice of the woman whose attention she'd craved yesterday could make her open her eyes. She had no intention of coming back. She would stay in that dark place behind her eyes, because there she could pretend that Jacqueline was coming home soon.

She felt Cecelia sit beside her, though Jasmine kept her head on Mae Frances's chest, still not moving, only thinking.

Her thoughts were random and peculiar. Was there a *Guinness Book of World Records* entry for kidnapping? Would Buster, the security guard from Bling, be the one to find Jacqueline this time?

Her head was spinning with questions and with the clipped, efficient commands of the security officers taking charge, making calls, doing all that they could to find the missing child.

And then.

"Mommy!"

Jasmine's eyes popped open as Jacqueline ran into the room past the security guards, past Reverend King, past her grandfather and father, and into her mother's arms.

"Jacquie! Oh, my God. Jacquie!"

Everyone in the room exhaled together as Jasmine held her daughter so tight she squirmed.

"Mom," the seven-year-old coughed. "I can't breathe."

That didn't matter to Jasmine. Her plan was to find a way to live her life without ever letting Jacqueline go.

Around them, there were cheers and pats on backs as Hosea knelt next to his wife and daughter.

Cecelia stood and shouted, "And all things, whatsoever ye shall ask in prayer, believing, ye shall receive!"

Jasmine didn't hear Cecelia. All she could do was say, "You're all right," over and over again.

"Mommy, why are you crying?"

It was only then that she relaxed her arms and sat back a bit. Her eyes took in her daughter—her beautiful daughter, who was wearing the same jeans and sweater that she'd had on yesterday.

"Where . . . where were you?" Jasmine asked.

Jacqueline grinned. "With Auntie Rachel. We had our own slumber party . . . me, Nia, and Auntie Rachel." She pointed toward the door.

For the first time, Jasmine noticed her. Rachel. She was standing at the door, wearing a sleeveless summer dress and a sweet smile on her face.

Rachel said, "My son just came back to the room and said they were all let go early, without breakfast, because a little girl was missing. I came down here because I thought we could help in the search. I had no idea the missing girl was Jacquie." Rachel placed her hand across her chest as if she was shocked.

"Jacquie's been with you?" Hosea asked.

"Yes, we told one of the chaperones," Rachel lied. "Jacquie begged to come with me and Nia and I thought since she was spending the night out anyway, it wouldn't be a problem."

Every eye in the room was on Rachel, though she didn't seem to mind.

"I'm so sorry, Jasmine, Pastor Bush."

Jasmine pushed herself from the couch. Slowly, she stepped unsteadily toward the door where Rachel stood and everyone anticipated this beautiful moment. It was no secret that the two women had been feuding: their back-and-forth duels had provided much of the excitement for the week. It had been enough to push their husbands and the Coalition's council to the edge.

But as all watched, peace had finally come—these two women would now be able to lay aside their differences and bond over their common ground—motherhood.

Standing right in front of Rachel, Jasmine stared into the eyes of the woman she'd sent to jail. And she thought about how bad she'd felt about taking Rachel away from her children. She thought about how she'd repented for that.

But that woman had come back and taken this battle to a low that had nothing to do with the election. This had not been about making sure her husband won the presidency. This had only been about torturing her. This had only been about payback.

Rachel kept her smile sweet, innocent. But in her eyes, she taunted Jasmine.

And Jasmine took her dare.

It was quick.

It was efficient.

She cocked her right hand, and with the torque movement she'd learned in boxing class, she connected with Rachel's jaw; the cracking of Rachel's bones echoed through the silent room. The impact made Rachel stumble back, one step, two steps, three steps, until she fell flat on her back.

Knocked unconscious. At least for the moment.

Chapter
TWENTY-THREE

R achel! Rachel!"
Rachel heard the voices, but they sounded like they were coming from far away. She squinted. Tried to get her bearings back. Slowly, she opened her eyes as the words grew louder. Why were these people screaming her name? Why was everyone standing around staring at her? She glanced around as she blinked back into focus. And what in the world was she doing on the floor?

"Are you okay?" Cecelia King knelt over her, lightly slapping her face.

"I . . . I'm fine," Rachel said, her hand immediately going to her jaw, which screamed with pain when she spoke. "What happened?" she asked as she tried to sit up.

Before anyone could answer, she looked over to see Hosea holding Jasmine back. The old lady that was always with them was also glaring at Rachel. Suddenly, everything came rushing to light.

She'd been coldcocked by this crazy trick.

"You hit me?" she yelled at Jasmine.

"I sure did," Jasmine spat. "And you're lucky that's all I did!" She was clutching her daughter. "How dare you take my child?"

"Mommy, I asked to go," Jacquie whimpered. "I'm sorry."

Rachel's first instinct was to get up and charge Jasmine like a raging bull. Rachel had changed, but not so much that she'd allow someone to knock her out and not retaliate.

"Oh, you have lost your mind," Rachel said, struggling to get up off the floor. She was just about to race over and rip that high-dollar weave out of Jasmine's hair when she noticed Cecelia helping her up. She looked around the suite. Every eye in the room was on her, including the police officers standing in the corner.

No, a catfight would only make them both look bad. Taking the high road would speak so much louder. Well, taking the high road and showing Jasmine what jail felt like.

"Officers," Rachel said, motioning toward the police, "I want this lady arrested for assault." She rubbed her sore jaw for dramatic effect. "You witnessed it. *Everyone* witnessed it and I want to press charges."

Hosea immediately turned to Rachel. "Rachel, that's not necessary."

"The hell it isn't! She hit me for no reason! I'm probably going to have to have surgery to repair my jaw. Come to think of it, not only do I want to press charges, but I'm going to sue you for damages as well!" she shot at Jasmine.

"Well, let me give you some more injuries to add to your lawsuit!" Jasmine said, charging toward her.

Hosea grabbed Jasmine and pulled her back. "Jasmine, calm down."

"Calm down! This woman deserves to have her throat slit for what she did! And I'm just the person for the job."

"Do you see this!" Rachel shouted to the officers as she stepped behind Cecelia. "Add terroristic threats to the charges!"

"Jasmine"—Hosea shook his wife—"Jacquie is safe and sound. There is no need to get out of control."

"Are you freakin' kidding me? This woman stole my child." Jasmine turned to the officers. "If anyone needs to be arrested, it should be her for kidnapping!"

"Kidnapping? I didn't kidnap anyone!"

By this point, tears were streaming down Jacquie's face. "Mommy, this wasn't like when the bad man had me. Auntie Rachel didn't kidnap me. I asked to go." Jacquie trembled as she spoke.

"She ain't your damn aunt!" Jasmine bellowed.

"Jasmine, you're scaring her." Hosea hugged his daughter tightly. "Sweetheart, it's fine. Mommy was just worried when she couldn't find you."

"I was playing with Nia." Jacquie sniffed. "She's my friend now."

"I would never hurt Jacqueline," Rachel protested. That much was true. Jacqueline had had a wonderful time. They'd popped popcorn and watched *The Princess and the Frog* until all three of them fell asleep. Of course, Lester had questioned why Jacquie was there, but Rachel had assured him that she'd wanted to come with Nia. "I told the chaperone that I was taking both girls because they were ready to go. I even left a note at the front desk," Rachel said innocently. She'd known Jasmine was going to blow a gasket, so she'd covered her bases last night and left a note to be delivered to the Bushes that Jacqueline was with her. She just didn't bother telling anyone that she'd asked that the note be given to the Bushes upon checkout.

Jasmine's nostrils flared as she glared at Rachel. Hosea gently patted his wife's arm. "See, honey, this was all a misunderstanding."

Jasmine snatched her arm away.

"Do you really think I would do anything to Jacqueline?" Rachel asked, feigning shock.

"I don't know what your crazy behind is capable of!" Jasmine said.

"Oh, we already know which one of us plays dirty," Rachel replied, her tone stiffening.

"Stop it!" Cecelia finally interjected. "The two of you just stop it! This is ridiculous." She glanced around the room at the twenty or so people enjoying the show. And with the commanding presence that seemed to accompany her every move, she stood tall, her voice firm. "The Coalition will not be reduced to these types of catfights." She focused her attention on Rachel. "I am sorry about your ordeal at the mall yesterday. But I was there and it was all a big misunderstanding." She turned to Jasmine. "Just like Jacquie's disappearance was a misunderstanding. The girl has told you it was her idea to go."

"But——" Jasmine began.

"No 'buts,'" Cecelia snapped. "This has gotten out of hand. We've never had this type of drama before," she couldn't help adding.

The officers sighed as if they had tired of the show. "Well, it looks like we're no longer needed," the taller of the officers said as he headed toward the door.

Rachel stepped in front of the officer to stop him. "No, you can't leave. I'm serious about pressing charges."

Jasmine spoke up as well. "And I want to press kidnapping charges, too."

Cecelia threw up her hands in exasperation. "No one is pressing any charges." She looked at the officers. "Thank you for your assistance, but everything is fine now."

Both Rachel and Jasmine looked like they wanted to protest, but the disgusted expression on Cecelia's face stopped them from saying anything.

As the officers and hotel security exited, Cecelia turned to the rest of the people in the room. "We have a busy day today." She shook her head like she was deep in thought. "And to be quite honest, I have some things to assess, so it would be best if everyone just returned to their rooms to get ready for the nominating meeting."

"Cecelia——"

Cecelia held up her hand to cut off Rachel. "Not now, Rachel. Just go back to your room."

Rachel didn't appreciate being treated like a child, but she didn't want to push her luck, so she swallowed and turned to Jasmine. "I really am sorry you were worried about your daughter." Rachel was actually sincere in her apology. She still couldn't stand Jasmine, but seeing her still tightly clutching her daughter, Rachel imagined how she would feel if she thought someone had kidnapped Nia. Especially if Nia had endured the tragedy that little Jacquie had gone through just a little more than two years ago.

Maybe she really had gone too far with this scheme.

"I never meant to scare any of you," Rachel added apologetically.

Jasmine took a step toward her. For a minute, Rachel thought she was going to plant another hook across her jaw, but Hosea was holding tightly to her right hand.

"As long as you are black and female, don't ever say another word to me," Jasmine said slowly and firmly. Then she grabbed her child tighter and walked out the door.

It didn't take much to scare Rachel, but the look in Jasmine's eyes let her know war had been declared. It was a good thing Lester was going to win because Cecelia had made it clear that she expected them to work together regardless of the outcome. And the way Jasmine just looked at her, it would've been hell working under her. Shoot, at this rate, there was no way they'd be able to ever work together at all.

Chapter
TWENTY-FOUR

It had taken two grown men to drag Jasmine away from her children. Well, not drag exactly, but Hosea and Reverend Bush had to spend long minutes convincing Jasmine that Jacqueline and Zaya would be safe while she was at the nominating session.

"They'll be here in the suite with Mrs. Sloss and Mae Frances," Hosea said over and over. "No one will be able to get to them."

"We'll even have lunch brought into the room," Reverend Bush told his daughter-in-law. "They won't leave until you get back."

Finally, Mae Frances pulled her aside and said, "Snap out of it, Jasmine Larson. Remember why you're here; we've put a lot into getting Preacher Man elected." So Jasmine smothered her children with good-bye kisses and told them that she wouldn't be away for long.

"I won't leave again, Mama," Jacqueline assured her. "Not even if Auntie Rachel and Nia try to come and get me."

"That ho ain't your auntie," Jasmine snapped, before she could even think about her words. But in the next second, she pulled her daughter close and covered her with more kisses, trying to wipe away the look of horror on Jacqueline's face.

Now, in her own suite, Jasmine paced back and forth, resisting the urge to call down to the children's suite once again. The moment Hosea had left her alone to take his shower, she'd begun making the calls, checking up on the children every couple of minutes.

"What? No! Earl said that he left to start his own church."

"He did. And he took quite a few of Reverend Wright's members with him. But according to what I've read, that didn't matter to Reverend Wright. He just wanted to get rid of Griffith—for improprieties. It looks like Reverend Wright tried his best to keep it out of the news for the sake of his church, but Pastor Griffith was taking money from athletes and other celebrities and helping them to launder money through the church."

"Are you kidding me?" Mae Frances pressed her hand against her mouth as if she were trying to hold her shock inside.

"It's true," Jasmine said. For the last few hours, exhaustion had held her hostage, not letting go. But now the aches of her weariness dissipated. Adrenaline surged through her, and she stood and she paced and she told the story.

"Pastor Griffith would take a ten-million-dollar check from someone, have them call it a tithe so that they could write the entire amount off, and then flush five million back to them in cash. And there were other schemes, too—money laundering for drug dealers."

"Oh, my God!" Mae Frances sat, stilled by the shock. "So . . . what does this mean?"

"It seems that his church is now under federal investigation for these same practices. He's been able to keep the story quiet because he keeps telling officials that he'll cooperate." Jasmine took a breath. "What I think is that he's looking for another place to put all of this money. He's betting that no one would look at the Coalition, especially if the ABC merged with the National Baptist Coalition."

Mae Frances shook her head. "You're losing me. What merger?"

Jasmine filled Mae Frances in on everything that Rachel had told her—about overhearing Cecelia with Coco, about what Lester Adams said about no one wanting the merger, and lastly about the article she'd read. "It was that article that I couldn't get out of my mind. About the merger and Pastor Griffith's connection to Cecelia," she said. "It was that article that made me search for more."

"And that's when you found out about the investigation?"

Jasmine nodded.

"But the merger, you said he was in it with Cecelia?"

"Yeah," Jasmine sighed. "That's the part I can't quite figure out. If he was in on the merger with Cecelia, why didn't he just back her?"

Mae Frances shook her head. "I don't know. Maybe he thought it would just be better with Hosea at the helm."

"Maybe." Jasmine nodded. "Maybe he felt that with someone like Hosea, the authorities would never look at the Coalition, especially if it had merged and was twice the size."

Mae Frances said, "They might have even chosen Hosea specifically."

"Exactly."

"A high-profile preacher who always does the right thing. No one would look at him. But if the law did come . . ."

Jasmine stopped walking, stood in front of Mae Frances, and nodded. "Hosea would be the one in charge of the Coalition. He'd be the one responsible. He'd be all up in this. And if he didn't do what Pastor Griffith and the Killer B's told him to do—"

"Wait!" Mae Frances held up her hands. "The Killer B's?" Her eyes were wide at the mention of one of the most notorious gangs in the country.

Jasmine nodded. "This whole investigation began because of the Killer B's and Pastor Griffith's connection to them."

"Oh, my God." Mae Frances shook her head. "I just can't believe this, Jasmine Larson."

Jasmine said, "I think that's where Pastor Griffith got all of the money. For the North and even the million that he used to cover me. I think much of the money is drug money."

Mae Frances pushed herself from the couch. "I've got to check this out."

"No." Jasmine grabbed her arm. She was shaking with fear. "You can't say anything to Pastor Griffith," she pleaded. "If only half of this is true, it's enough to—"

"I'm not going to call him, Jasmine Larson." Mae Frances

snatched her arm away. "Give me some credit." She walked toward the phone. "I need to make a call, though."

"To whom?"

"Jeremiah Wright."

Jasmine nodded. She could handle that; she felt safe with the call going to him.

It took Mae Frances a couple of calls to get through, but as Jasmine watched her talk to the reverend and then his son, she knew she'd been right. What she'd discovered was just the tip of what could be a disaster.

Though the phone was still pressed to her ear, Mae Frances fell onto the bed as if the burden of the shocking revelations was just too heavy to handle. When she yelped another "Oh, my God," Jasmine slowly took out the flyers that she'd made about Lester and Rachel from the envelope.

She began to rip them in half.

There was no way she was going to let Hosea win this election. The problem was, she couldn't go to him with this information, though. Hosea wouldn't be afraid; he would just tell Pastor Griffith that there wouldn't be any illegal activities going on while he was president of the Coalition.

No, Hosea wouldn't have any fear at all, and he'd tell Pastor Griffith that he wasn't scared.

That was okay. Hosea didn't have to be afraid; Jasmine had enough fear . . . and enough good sense not to mess with this, enough for the both of them.

As Mae Frances kept talking, Jasmine kept tearing the flyers . . . one by one, two by two, three by there. And she thought of new flyers that she had to make.

She only had a few hours to make it happen, but she was sure by the time morning broke, and the new flyers were read in the light of day, there would be very few who would vote for Hosea Bush as the president of the American Baptist Coalition. Merger or no merger.

And that was exactly the way Jasmine wanted it.

Chapter
THIRTY-FOUR

Now she knew how Michelle Obama felt on that brisk November day back in 2008. Rachel felt a mix of queasiness, anxiety, and eager anticipation. In just a few hours, the votes would be cast and she would officially become the first lady of the American Baptist Coalition.

But first, there was one other order of business.

I'm in front of the ballroom. CK on her way down. The text from Melinda had put the game plan into motion. Rachel kissed her kids, who sat in the living room of the suite watching *SpongeBob SquarePants*. They were oblivious to the fact that their lives were about to change forever. And Rachel liked it that way. She wanted her kids to have the best in life. Granted, she grew up in a pretty middle-class household, but she wanted her own family to know a life she only dreamed about.

And she was about to give it to them.

"Be good for the sitter, kids," Rachel said, heading toward the door, where Lester was impatiently waiting. "When we get back, we're gonna have a big celebration."

"What we celebratin'?" Nia asked.

"Daddy's getting a new job," Rachel said.

"Rachel . . ." Lester began.

Rachel stroked her daughter's hair. "Daddy is modest about his new position, but Mommy has enough excitement for us all."

"What's 'modest'?" Nia asked.

"You so dumb," Jordan said, not looking up from his PS2.

"No, I'm not, and I bet you don't know either."

"Okay, stop that fighting." Rachel shot them both warning glances. "If the sitter tells me there's been any fighting when I get back, you're in big trouble. Understand?"

"Yes, ma'am." Nia nodded.

Jordan just grunted. Brooklyn and Lewis were engrossed in a Fisher-Price piano.

"Sweetie, are you ready? It was your idea to get down there early," Lester said.

Rachel nodded as she scooted toward the door. Lester thought they were getting downstairs a little ahead of schedule just to get situated. But Rachel wanted to make sure they were front and center for the show.

By the time they made it downstairs, the show had already begun. Melinda was at the back of the ballroom, looking over some notes. Scott, the photographer, was behind the camera. Another lean, lanky man was pulling cords and cables across the floor. Cecelia was coming down from the stage and heading toward Melinda.

"Hey, why didn't you tell me we were getting some more media coverage?" Lester asked as they walked in.

Rachel feigned surprise. She didn't respond because she didn't want to outright lie to Lester any more than she had. "Wow, that's Melinda. Let me go say hello."

Rachel left her husband's side, but took her time getting over to Melinda. She wanted to give Cecelia enough time to get within earshot.

"Hey, Rachel," Melinda said as both Rachel and Cecelia approached. "Mrs. King."

"Hello, Melinda," Cecelia said, not bothering to acknowledge Rachel. The blatant diss was a slap in the face, and had she not known what was about to go down, she probably would've been angry.

"What are you doing here?" Rachel asked, leaning in to hug her.

"Oh, the tape with Cecelia's interview messed up. I would've called you, but I've been swamped. I just figured I'd see you here and—"

"Hey, sorry to cut you off, but we're thirty seconds out," Scott said.

"Sorry, Rachel," Melinda said, moving into place. "We're actually going live, so I'll just chat with you later."

"Yes, she'll chat with you later," Cecelia said with a haughty tone.

"Well, is it okay if we stand back and watch?" Rachel asked. She wasn't going to let Cecelia get under her skin. Payback was just seconds away.

"Yeah, but I need you to stand back and stay quiet," Scott said as he waved back Rachel and several other people who'd gathered around to watch.

Cecelia stepped into place with an air like she was about to be interviewed by Oprah.

"Standby, and three, two." Scott pointed a finger at Melinda.

"Good evening, Colleen. We are live at the American Baptist Coalition Conference," Melinda began. Cecelia stood confidently, just out of frame. Rachel wanted to rejoice at how the entire ballroom had literally gone quiet so that they could hear.

"The ABC is one of the largest religious organizations in the country. And it appears that they're about to get even bigger. NewsChannel Four has learned about a secret deal that the ABC is working that will merge this group with the National Baptist Coalition." Gasps filled the ballroom. Melinda turned to Cecelia, who stood in stunned disbelief. "With me now is Cecelia King, the current first lady of the ABC, who with her husband, Rev. Andre King, is responsible for this merger. Mrs. King, how does it feel to know that your group is about to become one of the most powerful in the country?" Melinda pointed the microphone at Cecelia.

"I . . . ah . . . I . . . where in the world did you get your information from?" Cecelia said, trying to pull it together.

"There has been a very public rivalry between the two groups, so it's big news that the two of you are coming together. Particularly in light of the fact that the NBC recently filed for bankruptcy and is accused of misappropriation of funds."

"Again, where did you get that information from?"

"Is it true or not?"

Cecelia's eyes darted over the room. Every person inside was staring at her, waiting for her answer. "Well, yes, but——" She could barely finish her sentence as chatter filled the room.

"I take it from the reaction here that many in your organization didn't know about this merger?" Melinda said.

"We sure didn't!" someone yelled from the front.

"We'll merge with them over my dead body!"

"What's going on? Are you really trying to merge us with those crooks?"

The photographer made wild gestures behind the camera, trying to get everyone to settle down.

"I——I thought this interview was about my plans for the ABC," Cecelia stammered. No longer was she the poised, sophisticated woman who could woo anyone. Now she looked like a teenage girl who'd been busted with a boy in her room.

"It is," Melinda said. "We're trying to find out if you plan to acquire the NBC's debt. What about all of the charges against the organization? Or was this a way for you to defraud the creditors the group owes as some people are alleging?"

"What?" Cecelia's face was aghast. "I never!"

"And you never will!" somebody shouted.

"Why are the details of the merger not being made public? Is there something you're trying to hide?"

"I resent your implications."

Melinda continued, "And is it true that you and your husband negotiated as part of the merger that the salary of the president of both organizations would be combined, making the president of the ABC the highest-paid president of any religious organization, at four hundred fifty thousand dollars a year?"

"What?" several people yelled as noise filled the room again.

Cecelia took a deep breath, then gritted her teeth. "I resent you waltzing up in here, trying to ambush me."

"I'm just asking simple questions—things our viewers want to know," Melinda said innocently.

"Really, I don't understand why anyone outside the ABC should care," Cecelia replied with arrogance.

"You don't?" Melinda said. "You're a tax-exempt organization. If you become the biggest religious organization, that's millions of dollars in taxes you'll be denying the American people."

Cecelia huffed. "Young lady, I'm going to ask you and your photographer to leave our meeting."

"But you were okay with us being here a few minutes ago."

"That's before . . ." Cecelia stopped talking as she realized all of the people in the room were staring at her. "This interview is over!" She turned and stormed away.

Melinda turned back to the camera. "Well, as you see, Cecelia King didn't want to answer our questions. But that doesn't mean we're going to stop asking. We'll stay on top of this story and keep you updated. Back to you."

Scott flipped his camera off and people began bombarding Melinda with questions. Rachel didn't want to stand around, just in case people wondered if she had something to do with the ambush. Lester was already eyeing her suspiciously, as if he knew she was involved.

Rachel didn't give him time to say anything as she turned to make her way to her seat to wait for the meeting to begin. Cecelia had made a hasty exit. Hopefully, she wouldn't return. But if she did, Rachel was confident that interview had cast enough doubt to steal Cecelia's thunder.

Chapter THIRTY-FIVE

Jasmine stood in front of the bathroom mirror and yawned. All she wanted to do was go back to bed and get the sleep that had eluded her all night. But that was not possible—she had to be downstairs with Hosea in just a few minutes. It was time for the Coalition to vote for president.

"Darlin'." Hosea banged on the door. "Are you almost ready? We're late."

"I'm coming," Jasmine said, though she didn't make a move, at first. After a few moments passed, she slowly walked into the lavatory area, closed the door behind her, lowered the lid on the toilet, and sat down.

The hem of her knit skirt rose slightly as she crossed her legs and glanced at her watch, wondering how much more time she could waste. Hosea wasn't going to stand for this much longer. Any second now, he'd be busting into the main part of the bathroom, demanding to know what was taking her so long.

But she needed the minutes to tick by because the more time she spent up here in their suite, the less time there would be for anyone to reveal to Hosea what she had done.

She covered her mouth as she yawned again, the evidence of just how tired she was. It had taken so much longer than she thought for her and Mae Frances to slip all of those flyers under the doors last night, but every moment had been worth it. As far as she was concerned, she was working to save her husband and children's lives. At least, that's how she looked at it by the time Mae Frances had finished talking to Reverend Wright last night . . .

Mae Frances had hardly been able to speak when she hung up the phone, but finally, she'd conveyed to Jasmine all that the reverend had told her. Reverend Wright did not know about Pastor Griffith's involvement with Hosea's election; he'd made that call to Hosea's boss, suggesting that Hosea run because Mae Frances had called him and he was such a fan of the Bush men.

"But he said for us to stay away from Earl." Mae Frances had almost cried when she'd told Jasmine that. "He said that there are definite connections between Earl and that gang and many believe he's not only laundering money, but dealing drugs."

Jasmine had sat down right next to Mae Frances. Together, they stared ahead, envisioning what their lives would be like if Hosea won the election.

"Jeremiah said that it would make sense for Earl to want this," Mae Frances continued with the bad news. "To get the gang involved in something bigger than his church—it would be easier to hide money. But he wasn't aware of the merger being back on. He said there had been a rumor that Earl was working with the Kings on trying to move the merger forward a couple of years ago, but because so many on both sides were against it, it was all so hush-hush. And Jeremiah was very surprised to hear that talks of the merger were back on."

"Are the Kings involved with Pastor Griffith and the gang?"

Mae Frances shook her head. "Jeremiah didn't know anything about that. He's not sure where Cecelia and her husband fit in, but he doubts that they would be involved in this. He said the Kings are all about power; they're money hungry, but he doesn't believe they would get caught up in anything too far out there— like drugs and money laundering."

"So." Jasmine squinted as if she was trying to think this through. "Maybe these are two separate things. We're trying to connect the dots, but maybe there's no puzzle."

Mae Frances nodded. "Maybe it's just about the Kings wanting the merger and Earl wanting a place to hide what he's doing. Maybe the Kings are not caught up in that at all."

"No," Jasmine sighed. "It looks like it's just Hosea who's caught up."

Mae Frances had taken Jasmine's hand. "Jeremiah said that if I have any proof of anything, I need to take it to Hosea and Sam—"

"No way," Jasmine said before Mae Frances could even finish. "I know my husband and father-in-law, and they'll try to fight it. They'll move forward with this election, they'll fight to win, and then they'll dare Pastor Griffith to mess with the Coalition. But I think it's too late, anyway. I think Griffith has probably already promised people things. And they won't care for a second how much of a stand-up guy my husband is."

Mae Frances nodded.

"I don't want Jacquie and Zaya anywhere near that gang. You've heard the stories," Jasmine said, leaving out how the gang was known for not even caring about women and children.

"But what are you going to do? This morning, Earl said that Preacher Man was edging ahead. He's always had the lead, but the way they've been working, even with Cecelia in the race, Hosea will win by a good margin."

Jasmine nodded, not surprised.

Mae Frances sighed. "You know why Hosea is so far ahead, right?" She didn't give Jasmine a chance to respond. "It's because of everything we did to make Rachel Adams look like a fool. Those people don't want her as the first lady—they don't want her as the face of the Coalition. They think she's young and dumb."

"She's not dumb," Jasmine said. "Trust that." She inhaled. "Rachel will be able to handle herself. She *almost* handled me."

"But she didn't, and we're going to win this thing. And then, Preacher Man will be caught up with . . ."

Jasmine had saved one flyer—just to show Mae Frances what her plan had been. "This was going to be my last shot before the election tomorrow," she told her friend. "This would have taken down the Adamses."

Mae Frances studied the flyer and the tears that were in her eyes a moment ago were replaced by a smile that Jasmine hadn't seen in a while. "Jasmine Larson," she said, "I've taught you well." But then her despair returned. "But this will guarantee that Preacher Man will win!"

Jasmine took the flyer from Mae Frances's grasp and did to it what she'd done with the others—she tore it in half and then in half again. "No one is going to see this. Instead we're going to make up a new one." Jasmine closed her eyes as if that was the only way she'd be able to tell Mae Frances what she had to do. "This time, the flyer will be all about me. And my days as a stripper . . . and . . . all the other things I used to do at that club."

There was a moment of silence before Mae Frances asked, "Are you sure?"

Slowly, her eyes fluttered open. "I have to. I have to make sure that Lester Adams wins. I have to protect Hosea."

So, that's what they'd done. After Jasmine had lied to Hosea, telling him that she was staying in the children's suite because Zaya wasn't feeling well, she and Mae Frances had made new flyers that exaggerated the story of Jasmine Cox, the stripper and high-priced call girl. And though she'd never been in jail, the flyer cited arrest after arrest, scandal after scandal. Then they'd printed up three hundred copies (because the center had run out of paper) and waited until after midnight to get them to as many rooms as they could. They'd had a good amount of flyers left over, but Mae Frances had destroyed them all.

There was no trace of their deception, no link between them and the flyers. And as Jasmine had laid her head on the pillow at just after four in the morning, her prayer had been that she'd done enough.

And in just about an hour, she would find out.

"Jasmine!"

Just as she expected, Hosea had barged into the bathroom.

"Are you okay in there?" he asked.

She stood, and even though the lid was still down, she flushed the toilet. Then she pressed her hand against her stomach and opened the door.

"I'm sorry, babe," she said, keeping her voice at a whisper. "My stomach is a little unsettled."

The annoyance that was on his face melted and he pulled her into his arms. "Darlin', you're just nervous."

"Yeah, I guess I am."

"Don't sweat this. It's going to work out the way God wants it to."

Jasmine nodded and Hosea clasped her hand inside his and led her into the bedroom. She grabbed her purse, took a final glance in the mirror, and prayed that God's plan and hers were exactly the same.

Jasmine was still holding Hosea's hand as they walked toward the ballroom. She tried to prepare herself for the glances and the whispers that she was sure would come her way; she just wasn't prepared for what she would say to Hosea.

Before she and Hosea even turned the corner, thoughts of the flyers that she prayed would seal Hosea's fate flew out of her mind. The hallway in front of the ballroom was packed with people, shouting. And in the narrow space of the hallway, their voices bounced off the walls, making it sound almost like a riot.

And in the center of the commotion was Rachel's friend Melinda. She was being bombarded with questions by members of the Coalition.

"How did you find out about the Kings' plans?"

"Who else is involved with this?"

"Can you do a full exposé to make sure nothing like this happens?"

From the questions that were being thrown at her, Jasmine knew that Melinda had done her job well. Now she was sorry that she had missed the show, but she'd had no choice. At least her reporting had taken away any attention that anyone had on the flyers.

Jasmine and Hosea pressed their way through the crowd, but inside the ballroom, the confusion continued. The aisles were filled with members, talking over one another, surprise on everyone's face. Onstage, Reverend Capers, the sergeant at arms, was trying to call the meeting to order, but no one seemed to be paying attention to the pounding of the gavel.

"I wonder what's going on?" Hosea whispered to Jasmine.

She shrugged, as if she didn't know, but at the same time, she scanned the space for the Kings, though it was hard to see anyone through the hundreds that filled the room. She did see Rachel, though, sitting in the front row, all prim and proper, with her eyes on Reverend Capers. It was as if Rachel was totally oblivious to all that was going on.

For the first time in hours, Jasmine smiled. Rachel created chaos, and then sat back and let it all unfold. If she didn't hate her so much, she just might like her.

Hosea led Jasmine down the center aisle, and few looked their way. The members were caught up with the merger; right now, they had little thought of the flyer that had appeared in their rooms this morning.

At the front, Hosea turned one way to greet Lester. She turned the other way and looked right into the face of Pastor Griffith.

"Good morning," he said, all smiles, all confidence.

It was hard for her to greet him back. Now that she knew what this man was all about and who he really was, she not only didn't want to have anything to do with him, she didn't want to talk to him.

But she had to act as if everything was the same. He was, after all, affiliated with the Killer B's. So she smiled, she nodded, and then she sat down and folded her hands in her lap.

With just a slight motion of her head, she turned the other way and glanced at Rachel, who was already looking at her. Rachel nodded, sending her a message. Jasmine nodded back, message received. They'd worked together for just twenty-four hours and it looked like they had brought Cecelia King and her husband down.

Hosea slipped into the seat next to her and unbuttoned his jacket. "You are not going to believe what happened," he said.

Her heart began to pound. Had Lester told Hosea about the flyers? Had she or Mae Frances made the mistake of putting one under the Adamses' door? Or had someone from their side showed it to Lester?

It had been so confusing last night. Mae Frances had been able to get a roster of who was staying in what room. But it was so much to digest and they had been tired . . . had they made a mistake?

"Cecelia King was just ambushed by a television reporter," Hosea said. "That's who's in the hallway. Turns out the Kings were trying to merge the ABC with the NBC and that's why Cecelia entered the race."

"Really?" Jasmine feigned surprise as her heartbeat slowed down to normal.

But she didn't get to say anything else. Reverend Capers was finally able to bring order to the room, and the Coalition members settled into their seats.

"We will now bring this meeting to order," the reverend said as he slammed the gavel against the podium.

Jasmine could barely breathe as another pastor went to the stage and led them in prayer. She didn't listen to the pastor's words, though; she had her own petition that she wanted God to hear.

After that, the conference parliamentarian took the stage and explained the voting process.

Finally, the parliamentarian said, "And now, as we prepare to vote, we would like to have the candidates go to the holding room. First, we have Lester Adams and his lovely wife, Rachel."

The Adamses stood, waved to the crowd, and the Coalition members responded with applause.

"Next," Reverend Capers continued, "Hosea Bush, and the beautiful Lady Jasmine."

As Hosea stood, he took Jasmine's hand and they both waved to the crowd. But this time, the applause was mixed with hisses and whispers.

Hosea frowned a bit, but led Jasmine through the side door. "I wonder what that was about?" he asked once they were outside.

Once again, Jasmine shrugged, as if she didn't know. But now that she was away from all of those people, she didn't want to think about what she'd done, she didn't want to think about what the members now thought of her and Hosea. All she wanted to do was get to that holding room, take her husband's hands, and pray until all the votes were in and tallied.

The Kings weren't in the room, but Hosea and Jasmine were. They sat at a corner table, their heads bowed in prayer. Hosea's father stood in the other corner, his own head down as if he was praying, too. For a moment, Rachel wondered why the senior Reverend Bush was not in the other room voting—but then she remembered, the Bushes had not been members of the ABC. Reverend Bush couldn't vote.

When the Bushes finished praying, Rachel stood to go over and talk to Jasmine. She wasn't in the room during the interview and Rachel was anxious to tell her how well it had gone. But Jasmine's odd expression stopped her in her tracks.

She didn't seem as excited as Rachel. She looked scared. Nervous. Worried. Maybe she was about to pull a trick out of the bag. Rachel hoped that wasn't the case because this last little bit of info she had on Jasmine, she was hoping she wouldn't have to use. Despite all her bourgieness, Jasmine seemed like she could be cool. In fact, she kinda reminded Rachel of herself—in about thirty years.

That's why she was hoping Jasmine didn't stab her in her back, because then she'd have to play this last card, and it wouldn't be pretty.

Rachel studied Jasmine from across the room. She was in some serious thought. Suddenly it dawned on Rachel. Of course Jasmine was worried. Cecelia might no longer be a problem, but Jasmine knew Hosea was about to lose to Lester. Naturally, she had cause for concern.

Rachel shrugged. *Oh, well, guess we won't be friends, after all,* she thought as she sat back down next to Lester, who had his head buried in a Bible. Jasmine was probably going to return to her old funky self after Hosea lost.

"I wish I had your confidence," Lester said, looking up to see Rachel sitting nonchalantly at the table.

"I told you, sweetheart, you got this."

"But Hosea . . ." Lester whispered.

"Is a good man. I'll give him that, but you're working with tradition. Sixty years, that's how long it's been since a Northerner was elected president. That's not about to change now. Not to mention the fact that you're the young breath of fresh air this organization needs. Those people in that room know that."

Before Lester could reply, the conference parliamentarian stuck his head in the holding room. "They're ready. The votes are tallied."

Nervous anticipation finally set in. Rachel placed her hand on her stomach to quell her nerves. This was it. She glanced over at the Bushes again. Dang, she really had Jasmine scared. If she hadn't started to kinda like Jasmine, she would've delighted in her fear.

Back in the auditorium, Rachel followed her husband to their seats. A couple of people gave her suspicious glares. Those were probably just Cecelia's people thinking she had something to do with the TV ambush.

Rachel kept her head high as she took her seat. Cecelia and Reverend King were the last to enter the room. Cecelia looked like she'd been crying. Her eyes were puffy and slightly red. No doubt she'd spent the last thirty minutes trying to pull herself together.

When Cecelia passed Rachel, she stopped and glared. If looks could kill, Rachel would definitely be six feet under. Rachel shrugged innocently, shook her head like she was so disappointed.

"Please, everyone, take your seats," the conference chairwoman said. "We need to get this meeting started." She sounded flustered, like the drama from the merger news had taken its toll.